CHOCOLATE FOR LILLY

carolineclemens.com

Also By Caroline Clemens

Into the Vines
Brie's Story
Someday
The Pilot Log
Autumn Quotes
String the Cranberries

Caroline Clemens

CHOCOLATE FOR LILLY

Chocolate For Lilly

For information about special discounts available for bulk
purchases, sales promotions, fund- raising and educational
needs, contact:

Clemensnovels
https://carolineclemens.com/

ISBN 978-1-37072-776-6
ISBN 978-1-64316-651-3

This novel is a work of fiction. Names, places, businesses,
events, buildings, people, and circumstances are either
used fictitiously, or are the author's imagination to build
creatively.

Dedicated to Pearl Marie Liphart.

CHOCOLATE FOR LILLY

Chapter 1

"We leave on Sunday," Jack Johnson announced after dinner on Tuesday evening.

"That will allow us time to pack our things in the trunks. What doesn't fit we sell or ship to Chicago," Ruth told her children at the table.

There was a few loud breaths amidst the turmoil of raised eyebrows and inward disturbed thoughts. No one but Mr. Johnson, their father, wanted to go to Chicago. He tried to entice them but failed. The only thing that seemed to bring a brightness in the group was the mention of a lake.

"Tell me more about the lake Father," said Emmaline.

"What do you care? Robert won't be with us. He's not moving and we don't get to go to North Carolina," said a distraught Fitz.

"Fitz, I'll not have you whining like a girl. Be

done with it," issued Mr. Johnson.

"Rose, read the paper to them. Read the areas I marked," he said and handed the paper to his eldest daughter Rose. Rose was a beauty with dark long shiny hair and deep set eyes. She was smart, too. He wanted her to achieve, maybe go to college.

Rose held the paper and spotted the areas her father had circled. "Railroads have become the vehicle for this revolution, and mobility, moving people and businesses to new frontiers. Is it endless? It appears so. The New York Central can take you and your family all the way to Ohio. There you can find a hotel right across the street from the train station on North Depot. The Murschel House has a dining room, reading room, bar and even a barber shop for personal convenience."

She looked up at her father as if to ask if she should continue. "Keep reading Rose."

"The Sandusky Star Journal-Register," said Lilly. Lilly was ten now and very proud of herself for reading the name of the paper. Her dark burgundy pigtails flopped around on her shoulders with her side to side head movements.

Ruth giggled. She couldn't contain herself after all the seriousness of the last month.

Petals barked and everyone looked to see what she wanted. It was just an acknowledgement of Mrs.

Johnson.

"Do go on Rose," begged Mr. Johnson.

While the servants cleared the table for dessert Rose quickly read ahead and began smiling rather quizzically, unbelievably. "It can't be," she whispered.

Smiling she continued. "It says here on the society page," she said and looked around the table at their faces.

"What? What?" asked Fitz. He was the most anxious and waited for her voice.

"Cedar Point President, George A. Boeckling, who turns sixty this year is celebrating the 25th year as head of Cedar Point. He has made Cedar Point what it is today! He is known as a "master showman and supreme egotist.""

"So?" asked Fitz.

"He has been elected president of Third National Bank," continued Rose.

"And, I'm waiting for the good part, sister," said an anxious Fitz who was fourteen with blonde curls that needed to be cut.

"Cedar Point has the largest bath house in the world," said Rose. She paused as she knew what was coming.

"Oh, lovely. We can all go swimming in the lake on our way to Chicago," replied Emmaline.

Ruth smiled. "I heard there is a steamer that

takes you over to the island or peninsula."

Rose looked at Fitz. "The Leap Frog Railway is the longest and biggest scenic railway costing $45,000 when it was built in 1918.'

"Leap Frog? How high is it sister?" he asked.

"Amazing Fitz! It takes you up seventy feet above the ground all around with curves and then returns to a station."

"Oh boy, I can't wait Father. How fun!" Fitz couldn't contain his excitement. He swirled around the room like he was going through the air and then jumped up and down. His mouth made swooshing sounds like a small locomotive.

"There is animals, trapeze artists, tumblrs, and diners. The Hotel Breakers is also open. You can go by boat or automobile over to the island or peninsula for the day or stay at the hotel, it says," said Rose.

"We will be staying at the Murschel House for three or four days and spend two days at the park. I read where a lion named Miss Adgie escaped one year and traveled down the midway. They later found her sunning herself near Lake Erie." Jack Johnson knew that one would get their attention. He looked around the table at the all big eyes.

"We have much to do and everyone must help. You will want to say goodbye to your friends, the Stephens included. Maybe we will have dinner with them on Saturday before we leave. We'll say goodbye then," remarked Ruth Johnson. She wasn't sure how well this move would go. They were going by train and model "T's" and she was positive something or someone was bound to get lost.

On Saturday night the air was light and casual. Neither of these families wanted it to be sad or sullen. The children listened to music from the radio and played with the animals. The adults separated into different rooms after dinner. Ruth and Mary began discussing her trip to Sandusky and finally, on to Chicago.

"I'm jealous Ruth, I wish I was leaving all this chaos of the city. The joints that have risen since Prohibition play music all night long it seems," said Mary.

"Mary, where do you think I'm going? I've heard Chicago is one wild town filled with vaudeville and jazz joints. They might even have more speakeasy clubs than New York, though, that seems impossible," Ruth pondered.

"Times are changing Ruth, very fast. Women can vote now and I've seen quite a few of them smoking at the club we visited with friends. Nobody bothered them at all," Mary exasperated.

Ruth acknowledged her friend. They both voted and admitted that it made them feel powerful.

"Women have been hidden for a long time, Ruth. Charles tells me these things. Him being the newspaper man, he knows everything. Did you read about Nelly Bly?" asked Mary.

"I did. She died this winter but her story came out about what she did. She exposed the mental wards for some of their preposterous behavior towards women. She pretended to be an insane woman by faking it. They believed her and then she investigated what they were doing to women inside. And she did this for ten days!"

"Incredible. You know she also operated a business in the milk container industry and invented a new one or fixed it or something. She holds a patent, now that's one fine lady. I leave the ambition for my son and husband. They are so much alike," said Mary.

"Yes, Mary, me too. I'm afraid I'm so busy even with my servants I'm not sure what I'd do. Though, I love the piano and may have Elizabeth teach me how to play," said Ruth.

"That would be a fine thing to do. With all the children and keeping them on the right track, well, all your time is used up," replied Mary.

"Emmaline has spurned an interest in tennis and I told her I'd play with her. I'll have to learn that sport once we get to Chicago," said Ruth.

"It looks like fun. Robert has been playing at a club they just opened. He's getting pretty good, at least he tells me so," replied Mary.

Meanwhile, out in the barn Emmaline and Robert looked over the paper that Rose had read aloud about what to see and do at the amusement park. Emmaline skimmed the pages until she came upon a headline that scared her. She read it out loud, "Orphanage Burned to the Ground."

"Oh no!" cried Robert.

"What about the children?" she asked herself and Robert.

"Read it Emmaline. What happened?"

She stopped. It was there in the first paragraph right in the second sentence. Unbelievable.

"Tell me, tell me Emma!"

"Robert," she looked up at him and swallowed before she continued, "they all died. They all died," Emmaline spoke the words softly and then her vision escaped her and she fell back. Robert went to her side.

"Emmaline, Emmaline." While he waited for her to come around he glanced over at the paper and read it himself. 'The fiery blaze scorched the facility that held twenty five children of all ages late last night as screams were heard blocks away. Charred remains were all that was left as it burned to the ground while most of them slept. A few burned bodies were found trying to open windows and escape.' He stopped and laid down next to his sweet friend Emmaline.

Chapter 2

Emmaline Johnson surely had to be the prettiest girl I'd ever seen. I was the lucky one. Our families had summer homes beside each other in the mountains of North Carolina. It took a week to get here by automobile and we'd arrived in time to read another announcement about peace. My dad placed the paper on the wooden kitchen table while we unloaded the car and then placed our trunks up in the bedrooms.

Our summer homes were newer and larger than our residences up north in the city of New York. A couple years before Emmaline's father and my own had constructed homes near the mountains of North Carolina, side by side. They told us it made it easier for the crew to bring supplies and cut costs, too. I was just glad to play with the large family. There was always something to do with exploring the land taking up most of our time.

It was June 29th, 1919 and we'd arrived for the summer just outside of Boone, North Carolina right in the mountains. Unbelievably, the automobiles made the trip without faltering, though, my body was still jumping when I laid down at night to sleep, at least for the first two nights. Mother managed to make us lunch after putting away the staples she'd obtained in town. When Father finished he picked up the paper and read the headlines, "A League of Nations Formed at The Paris Peace Conference."

"I don't know what I'm more excited about Charles, the war being over or women getting the right to vote?" asked my mother. I knew this was going to be another post-war conversation turned on its side so mother could talk about women getting to vote in the next election. Why did she want to vote anyway? Oh, I knew that answer and I knew not to ask her, else I'd get a lecture two hours long. Something about suffering or rather a Suffragette movement which lasted decades.

I politely asked, "May I be excused? I'd like to go see the Johnson's place and see what Fitz is doing today."

"Robert, you may. I've invited them for dessert later, so be sure to come home and clean up," said Mary Stephens. I looked out the kitchen window towards the other house and saw Fitz on the front porch.

"Okay mother, certainly." I ran out the back door, and was halfway down the steps when the screen slammed shut. My mother and father, Mary and Charles Stephens, would spend most of the afternoon discussing the peace conference following the war that ended the previous year on November 11th, 1918. They'd had family members that served their respective country and died in battle over in Europe. The war had taken a toll but businesses were looking prosperous now and his printing place in New York City was barely able to keep up with the growth. He was even considering the addition of radio very soon. It was another way to get the news out, keep people interested, or informed. They had met the Johnson's who lived on the same street and became friends. Jack Johnson had several trades like banking, spirits and winemaking. He came from a line of farmers who originally lived in Pennsylvania, then migrated to North Carolina. The very land their new houses lay upon was given to him by his family. He sold Charles Stephens the lot next door, well, fifty acres anyway. Jack's wife Ruth was a sweet lady who had four children, two pets and numerous servants. She'd had a miscarriage after giving birth to Fitz who had followed Rose. When she lost the third baby her husband Jack took them to the orphanage on the edge of town and proceeded to find his wife a new baby. He had no other way to console her. He didn't know how. They named the baby Emmaline and two years later Ruth had another child whom she named Lilly. This summer place would offer breathing room and freedom for the family to spread their adventurous wings within the mountains and rivers and expansive views. Jack and Charles had each found an apprentice for which they had taught over the last year to run their respective businesses. This is how they would leave for two months to be down in the mountains. They decided they would indeed spend time discussing future ventures. With the advent of the automobiles more things were possible, including places to visit and the availability of customers.

By the time I arrived at the wooden front porch Fitz's three sisters were there, too. Of course, the only one I really noticed was Emmaline. She had two pigtails, one on each side with ribbons flowing down alongside the curls that matched the sash she wore around her waist. These vivid colors made her appearance overdressed in the mountains. I couldn't decide what was more stunning, the view expressed out across the valley for miles and miles, or Emmaline grinning at me with her smile that stretched from ear to ear, make that pigtail to pigtail?

How could a girl be so cute? Or beautiful? I wasn't sure and being eleven didn't help. All I knew was that she and I would be together all summer long, each and every day.

Ruth yelled out, "Take Petals with you!"

"All right, mother," replied Rose. Rose was the oldest and had the longest, thickest black hair. It was rather shiny, too. She was thirteen, while Fitz was eleven with blonde curly hair. My Emmaline was nine, and Lilly, her baby sister, was seven years of age with hair the color of a dark burgundy sweater. Robert had never seen anything like it. These were his friends for the summer, the whole colorful bunch of them.

"Have you met Petals yet?" asked Lilly.

"No, I haven't. Did you just get her?" he asked.

"Yes, we did about a month ago. She's a cocker spaniel who loves to play. We'll take her with us. She'll be a good sport I just know it!" Emmaline gave Robert the explanation.

"Can we bring London?" asked Lilly.

"Most certainly not, he'll run away. We would never find him as he's an indoor cat," Fitz said to Lilly.

"Maybe I should stay here with London," Lilly pondered.

"No Lilly, the cat will be fine. You come and

explore with us. We are going to need each other to remember the way back through the woods.

"Don't worry, we will be just fine. My dad used to take me to a cabin in New York and we hiked for miles and miles," said Robert.

"Really? Miles and miles?" asked Fitz.

"He taught me ways to make sure you come back to the same location alive!" answered Robert.

"Such as?" Rose was insistent.

Quickly, I gathered my thoughts. I needed to impress this crowd waiting on my next sentence. "There's a few easy ways, the first is to follow a creek and come back the opposite way, obviously. The second is to leave a trail of something like food or crumbs but I don't like that one because it may draw in wild animals. Finally, you can break branches ever so often at a certain height, then follow that back. Which one do you like?" He waited for their answer.

"I like the creek one! Because there's a creek right over there," exclaimed Emmaline. She pointed in the direction of where she saw the water flowing as they pulled up the long drive earlier in the day. We followed her pointed finger and they all decided we both had the right idea. After all, they didn't want to get lost on the very first day at their new summer homes.

Fitz eyed his friend and gave him a knowing

smile. They were the boys on this venture, they would protect the girls. While Fitz had the curls, Robert had straight dark blonde hair and wore it short preferable to a military style. It was short at the sides and back with a cropping of hair on top. He did look dashing for an eleven year old and seemed the smartest with his knowledge of nature and outdoor things. Robert even knew what he was going to be when he was a man.

"A botanist is what I'll be and study," he said proudly for all to hear.

The gang of four with the cocker spaniel named Petals hurried out on the natural grass in front of the house. Rose spoke up, "I know what that is because we learned it in school. You want to study nature, things that grow in the wild or garden."

"Yes, but to be specific it is the study of plants, not of animals or fish."

"I don't know what I want to do. Am I supposed to know that Robert?" asked Emmaline.

"Emmaline, you can be whatever you want to be if you are not a mother."

She giggled. "Actually, I'd like to be both.

He just looked at her and stared. He didn't know what to say. He'd have to ask his mother. Maybe he should have listened to his parent's conversation about women and voting. How could a woman have children and a position or study at once?

"Can I do that Robert?"

"Probably not at the same time. Who would take care of the children?"

"You have a point. I guess the governess or maids or as some refer to them, nannies."

"I don't know but I suspect you should get your position or business first."

"Business." She repeated the word out loud. She picked up the day old newspaper that Robert had brought with them.

He looked at her again until Fitz caught him deep in thought.

"I don't think the liquor business is right for her, Robert."

"Maybe Robert will teach us something about all this nature!" exclaimed Rose. "Then we can figure out what we will be someday." The kids sighed not knowing what they would be some day but Robert had them thinking about it and this gave them pause.

Petals began barking going around in circles. Instantly they saw what was causing the commotion. It was a snake, a big black garden snake.

"Nothing to worry about! Because he's so big he eats mice and my mom likes that then she doesn't find so many in the pantry. That's what she tells me anyhow," Robert informed his pals.

"Let us run to the creek and let him be!" Lilly exclaimed.

As soon as the kid's party reached the creek it would be too enticing to put their toes into the water and so they did. The white feet and ankles felt the likes of pure clear cold mountain water which ran briskly hitting the banks escaping the mountain hibernation. Smiles from attempts at new adventures and conquering the wild outdoors were worn that June day in the mountains of Carolina at their new summer home.

"Is this creek big enough to fish? Do you know Robert if any fish live in here?" asked Fitz. He really wanted to know for some reason. He heard about people fishing but didn't where or how they did it. He was a city boy. He read newspapers that Roberts's dad, Charles Stephens printed.

"Well, I believe not. This is from the mountains over yonder, very cold and somewhere probably spills into a lake. Now, if we could find that lake we'd be in luck," Robert gave his friend the best explanation he could muster up. He'd been to the big lake in New York but never in Carolina. He figured the concept had to be the same. He could ask his dad. His dad knew everything about everything.

"I know. I know. Possibly, there might be a catfish. I don't know why they call them catfish but they live everywhere, rivers, lakes and creeks," said Rose. "Someone at school caught one."

"We'll keep our eyes looking for fish, but we'll probably catch a frog first," Fitz offered up.

The children followed the meandering creek for a couple hours before deciding to turn back. They had gone into the woods but kept close to the creek. Against the current is what Robert told them, and, of course, they believed every word he spoke on that first day in Carolina.

When they arrived back at the Johnson's house DJ, the English butler from Canada, told them the Stephens would join them for dinner and dessert would be served later at the Stephens house. Robert wondered what their chef might be cooking today. He was hungry. Lilly informed Robert that the chef was Irish and she couldn't understand a word he said, but it sounded so nice. He liked to make meat pies and grew cabbage and potatoes. Robert's stomach growled.

While the children had ventured out today and explored their new surroundings: creek, woods and all, Garrett, the chef and horseman, Deuce, had been out shooting birds for dinner in addition to what had been purchased in Boone before their arrival this morning. The servants who worked for the Johnson's came with them from the north and stayed in Carolina with them for the summer. They assured the family they were up for the adventure.

Tonight was going to be a celebration after the long week of travel. Tomorrow the garden would need tending and the chickens would be put in their area and fed. Francis the gardener was a Frenchman who brought his wife along. She was expecting a baby so would not be doing any difficult work this summer. She said she'd help clean and fix the vegetables for Garrett in the kitchen. Deuce was well trained in his horses, rode well and could handle many an odd job. He'd left the south in his youth and had been working for Mr. Johnson and his carriages right up until the model T explosion. Mr. Johnson still had horses but had purchased several cars so his job was varied. This made him a very useful employee.

DJ, the butler had to expand his duties for the summer house. He and Elizabeth, the English nanny were married and handled the children, the guests, and many of Mr. Johnson's business employees with their needs. The couple was younger and had inherited these positions from his mother and father who returned to their home country when the war broke out. They missed them terribly but wanted no part of the war as they had just been married. They, also, to the benefit of the children adored Ruth's four beautiful children. Already, Elizabeth had begun sewing dresses for the girls much to their delight. The three charming young ladies had matching frocks from time to time which they paraded for the family to view.

Fitz quickly washed up and went to find London the cat. He found him and cuddled the furry pet while he purred. London let him stretch him all around his neck and shoulders. This gave him a sense of warmth or good feeling from his small pet whom he loved.

Dessert at the Stephens was followed by the fantastic meal put together in such short notice from the Irish chef Garrett at the Johnson's. He made meat pies from the birds caught earlier in the day and a cabbage stew accompanied by fresh bread he had bought in town. He knew there would be no time to bake bread with the unloading of suitcases and supplies. He'd also bought some spirits and beer in town in addition to what Mr. Johnson brought from his factory up north. He didn't want the two families to run dry as he knew they would eventually make new friends and invite them over. He remembered that other families from their businesses had places down south and spent the summers here near the lakes and mountains. It sure was breathtaking, almost as sweet as his homeland. Nothing was as beautiful as Ireland, he declared. Nothing.

While the children played together in the large oversized family room the adults gathered together in a sitting room off the kitchen. It had views of the mountains beyond and one could look out the picture window which already had plaid curtains adorning the landscape. Charles poured himself and Jack a scotch while he offered the ladies an after-dinner wine. No one declined.

"Thank you Charles," replied Ruth.

"You're welcome. I'm so delighted we are all here together. I know Robert appears to love it already. He and I have done our share of hiking in the mountains. He started very young and seems to enjoy it so," said Charles to the group of four.

"Oh, yes. Rose tells me he proclaimed his future trade to be that of a botanist. He rather impressed my crew with his knowledge of the outdoors this afternoon. I'm sure everyone will feel safer with him along on their escapades," returned Jack.

"I know I will," said Ruth.

"We must give the children a couple maps of the place. That way if there is confusion or misplacement when out in the woods they will have a chance to return, though, Charles has taught Robert that many a times," Mary replied.

"I bought one in town at the store. We will keep it handy for all of us to use," Ruth answered.

"Great, I'll make some hand copies that will be easier for the children to read. That way if they do get lost they can find the creek or certain landmarks," said Charles.

Pearl entered the room and asked if anyone needed anything. She was the Stephens only help. She'd been with them before Robert was born. Her only job was to assist Mary with anything she needed like cooking, cleaning or caring for Robert when he was a baby and toddler.

The adults declined any needs and wished her a good night sleep.

"Good night. I'm sure I'll be asleep on the count of three," said Pearl and added, "tomorrow will be busy for everyone with the unpacking."

"Robert and I will be helping with that. See you in the morning Miss Pearl," Mary said politely.

Ruth stood up, "I'm going to check on the children to see how tired they might be."

When she appeared in the doorway the children didn't look up. She saw the girls playing house and the boys rolling marbles towards the wall. The girls had their dolls and the dog Petals lay next to them. It looked as though tea was being served. No one looked tired but she suspected when they lay their heads upon pillows tonight, sleep would find them quickly.

Charles poured the adults a second drink as they talked about summer and plans for it. With the war over Charles told them people would be spending more money and sales of all sorts should increase. Jack told them with the automobiles selling like hotcakes he suspected more businesses would be needed offering more income for everyone. They all agreed happier and more prosperous times were coming, though they were already in the black on their accounts.

The 2nd day after their arrival was the true beginning of summer. Deuce, the horseman and caretaker of the cars had set about putting iron stakes in the ground out back of the barn. He told the kids, namely Fitz and Robert, he would show them a game of skill they could learn and practice. They could play this and claim a winner each and every time. He went back in the barn and came out with several old horseshoes.

"Help me bring a few more of these out here boys and I'll show you what you can do."

They ran inside and looked around until they found several of the old horseshoes. Then they ran back outside to join Deuce and learn his game. He showed them and made it look real easy curling the post with the very first one he threw.

"Wow, you got it, just like that. This must be

easy," shouted Fitz.

He picked up one and swung his arm back and followed through and let go. He let go way too late and up in the air went the horseshoe.

"Watch out! It might hit you," screamed Robert.

Quickly, Fitz ran for cover, then started laughing. "It looked so easy, let me try that again."

"Wait boys, let me give you a couple tips. I don't want you knocked out and lying on the grass from a game of horseshoes!" lectured Deuce.

The boys worked on developing their horseshoe skills, tossing the iron shoe farther and farther away, as they backed up. It took time rendering more control to keep the piece at a low toss but finally after a couple of hours both seemed to be acquiring the skill. About this time little Lilly came around the corner with a jug of lemonade. She'd helped Miss Pearl make it in her kitchen. She liked Miss Pearl because she didn't do things for you, she had you do them. Lilly got to squeeze the lemons after she'd sliced them with a knife. Her own mother would never let her handle such an item for fear she might cut herself. She even got to bring the glass jug out here all by herself and she was only seven.

Lilly wore a very big smile as she set the jug down on a table just outside the barn. She told them to wait that she would be right back with the glasses.

Miss Pearl gave her a tray with four glasses and a dozen peanut butter cookies. Carefully, Lilly carried the tray outside and down the steps. Then she walked slowly back behind the barn where the boys were playing. She liked the new place and this state of Carolina. Of course, not being in school helped too. She didn't miss school not one bit. She was too busy playing. She was going to ask the boys when they would go exploring again. She definitely wanted to be a part of that.

She set the tray down and saw the boys looking at a piece of paper. "What's that Fitz?"

"Lilly, we have a map!" exclaimed Robert.

"A map of what?" asked Lilly.

"A map of our next adventure," added Fitz.

"Tell me."

"Look. Here we are," said Robert. He pointed and showed Lilly where she stood on the map.

Her eyes looked in amazement.

"And this is where we are going," said Fitz. Then he traced a line away from her place on the map.

"Do you see where the lake is?" asked Robert.

She saw it and smiled. "How long will it take to get there?"

"Not sure, yet. Maybe half a day or less. If we go, then we go early, okay?"

"That sounds like a plan. Let's go tomorrow,

then if it's a super place to play we can go again," Fitz instructed.

Lilly said she was going to tell the others. She was sure Emmaline and Rose would love the idea. She probably should tell Elizabeth, their nanny, or maybe she'd just tell Garrett, the chef, so he could pack them a lunch. Organization was definitely her skill; she decided she'd plan the whole thing. She'd have Deuce make sandwiches and pack the bag that supplied water when you were hiking. She'd also have the boys leave a map for Elizabeth, the nanny, so someone would know exactly their whereabouts. She'd tell her mother the plan so she wouldn't be worried and she'd explain how long they would be gone. She told Rose and Emmaline the plan and later the boys. It was set for tomorrow at the crack of dawn, right after the rooster 'cackled her song' in the fresh morning air.

The children walked abreast of each other through the field in front of the two houses. The boys had the map out, giving it another look over, and adjusting their location while advancing their sites ahead of them. Deuce had looked at the maps with them yesterday. He kept more than a few horses in the stables and showed them the bridles. He said he needed to know in case he had to retrieve them by horse later in the afternoon. One always had to use caution he warned them. Actually, this gave Fitz relief as he knew Deuce was as capable and adroit as anyone when it came to finding someone. He'd been riding horses a long time. They assured him they'd be home by dinner time.

Mr. Charles Stephens gave Robert a timepiece and kept one himself. This amulet had been given to him by his father before he died. They synced the pieces. He quietly and sternly told his son that while this domain belonged to them now, it was not without dangers. He must return and on time.

"I'd like to see your faces around four o'clock but I will send out a search party at five o'clock if you're not home," said his father. "I know you're going swimming at the little lake, be careful and don't lose track of time."

"We won't. I mean I won't. Everyone knows how to swim, they told me they learned last summer when they went to the Atlantic Ocean."

"Yes, their dad told me as such," he replied. "Have fun, see you at four or five o'clock."

While the children were gone the gardener, Frances from France, made good on his promise to build a gazebo in front of the larger house which belonged to Mr. Johnson. Both families could easily use it and from the location one could see the Mountain View even more than their front windows.

The equanimity that could be felt looking at all that beauty reminded him of where he grew up in the valley along the river.

He was also busy preparing areas around the homes for plantings, trees and such. *The temperament and seasons might even be like his own mother country,* he thought. Though he was in the mountains, the surrounding area made him feel at home. He wondered to himself if the owners might need someone to stay on year round down here and keep the place open. The horses were staying, maybe he should think about being the caretaker. He'd have to ask Mr. Johnson.

Once the boys had the map all figured out they instructed the others to fall in line. They were going further today than a couple days ago. By rough estimates it would take about an hour and a half to reach the small lake. Maybe it wasn't small after all. There were two lakes, an enormous one and the one they were headed for, both fed by the same river from the mountains. He wondered who made this crude map as it was hand drawn. Probably, he figured, the persons who sold his family the land. He didn't know who that was. His dad didn't know the people either. Mr. Johnson might know because his family was originally from these parts. That's how he obtained the land in the first place.

Robert forgot to tell his friend Fitz that a railroad track was another way to go hiking and return to your original spot. He definitely figured there was no tracks around these parts, especially in the mountains. They were on their own and it felt good in a way like an explorer. He hoped his family and Emma's came here every summer. Forever. He was having the best time playing in the barn chasing kittens and the new game he learned from Deuce called horseshoes. Deuce promised the kids he would teach them to ride horses starting next week after everything was put away. He would make sure he had enough supplies. He told them they would all ride to the lake and let the horses have a bath. *That sounded like fun* thought Lilly.

Fitz led the way, followed by Rose and Lilly. Emmaline made sure Lilly kept in pace and didn't stray off the path looking for frogs or a special flower to pick. She turned to Emmaline and pointed at the sun rising up behind them. Emmaline quickly looked and said to Lilly, "Yes, Lilly, it's going to be a beautiful day! Do you remember how to swim?"

"Emma, I think so and if I don't I can float," Lilly said.

"That's right. But just in case you should stay by my side, okay?" Emma directed.

"Sure big sis, anything you say," Lilly said and

hurried to catch up the pace.

Emmaline turned around and saw Robert who smiled at her. She smiled back and kept hiking towards their destination. No one frolicked in the creek. They were going to a true swimming hole, a lake filled with cool mountain water. No one suspected how really cold it was going to be. But they were kids, they could handle it.

Robert followed the group and held onto the back sack filled with lunch supplies and a canteen of drink. He was pretty sure it was lemonade made by Pearl. This made him smile. He'd known Pearl since he was born. She helped out the family in so many ways. She was a built in playmate for him, too. Pearl was a white woman who his mother told him had lost her family to some illness that wiped them all out. They all died, he remembered, but her. She was lucky, but, really, not as lucky as she had no one. His mother took her in, let her take care of him by cooking and cleaning. That's the way it was. His father was gone for long periods of time. He was a newspaper man, the editor. He sometimes had to be gone all night or very early in the morning. People wanted to read the paper with their coffee that they drank in the morning. Robert's mother told him, he was successful, in that his paper was growing and he was making lots of money. Pearl, she said was a

God send in that she came along at the right time for everyone. His mother was glad to help her out. She thought someday she might go find another husband and start another family but that didn't happen as yet. Robert was glad she was still around. He would hate to see her leave.

The group didn't stop and walked through fields of grass in meadows leading up to the mountains. They walked through woods and did not encounter any wild animals that they could see anyway. It seemed to be a quiet morning made just for them. When they completed the walk through the denser woods and came back towards the sunrise they saw the lake.

Fitz saw it first. "There she is, yeah!" He ran and ran and the others followed. Along the lake on this side was a grassy area with rocks and a couple dead trees laying on their side. The lake was calm and bigger than they suspected. Fitz immediately wondered how deep it was. He better ask Robert that question. Certainly, he would have an idea. He'd seen these kinds of lakes he'd told the group when they discussed how to get back safely when hiking.

All the kids ran to the water's edge and stood admiring this lake in the mountains.

"Pretty," said Lilly.

"It's so cold," said Rose when she touched it

with her hand.

"I'm first," said Emmaline. She quickly took her shoes and socks off and stepped in about a foot out, just enough to cover her feet and wet her ankles.

"I'm next," shouted Robert.

"Robert, how deep do you think the middle?" asked Fitz.

Robert looked out towards the middle and gave Fitz his best speculation. "Fitz, you see the top of that mountain over there?" Robert pointed to the highest peak he could see.

"Yes, I do," replied Fitz.

"That's your answer," answered Robert.

Fitz looked perplexed.

"Brother," said Emmaline when she figured it out, "Bobby is telling you it's over your head!" She laughed and laughed. The others joined in.

Fitz didn't think it very funny. He felt responsible as one of the big boys on this trip.

"Fitz, you look worried. Why don't you test everyone here in the shallow parts to make sure they can swim? Mother would love that idea," Emmaline instructed.

"Emmaline, you were born with wits, more than anyone I know. That's an excellent idea. When you are ready to go swimming, come and see me first. I'll test you to make sure as we want everyone to make it home today. Deuce told me he's serving chicken and dumplings and peach pie," Fitz said with confidence, thanks to Emmaline and her great idea.

Emmaline and Robert came to Fitz's side first and asked to be tested. He watched both of them swim like frogs and passed them off, after they got used to the cold water. Then the others lined up and proceeded to be checked off by Fitz. Little Lilly decided that Fitz, too, needed to be checked off. She asked him to swim two laps for her so she could see that he was strong and able.

"Passed," she proclaimed.

No one complained about the cold waters of the lake in Carolina. The party became refreshed and invigorated as they swam for a very long time. Later on they enjoyed the food and drink, which was lemonade made by Pearl.

"Robert, I just checked your timepiece," said Emma.

"What time is it?" he asked.

"I think it's time to go," she repeated.

"Look at the shorter piece. Where is it?" he asked.

"It's on the number two, Roman numeral two," she shouted.

"And the longer, skinnier piece is where?" Bobby asked.

"Well, let me count," she said and proceeded to count out loud. He could hear her.

Finally, she stopped at ten, the Roman numeral expressed as a large X. "It's at ten!"

"It's one fifty. Time to go, right now!"

"That will get us home between four and five if we leave now," she said.

"Yes, if nothing happens along the way," said Robert. The kids quickly put clothes back on over their swimming trunks and makeshift bathing suits. Hurriedly they gathered any other belongings, tucked them in the sack and off they were filing away in single file.

"I have to go to the bathroom," cried Lilly.

Fitz stopped in his tracks. They weren't even very far away from the lake. "Why didn't you go when you were swimming?" he asked.

"I didn't think to do that," she cried. Then she began crying because she was going to make them late.

"Lilly, honey, don't fret. You won't make us late. Look over there. It's a landing with some grass and trees, just a bit away from the creek," Robert said, fixing the situation.

"Let me walk her over there," Rose said.

The pair walked away from the group, but still where they could see them. Rose thought it funny that there was a wall right next to the trees but then she saw something even funnier. "Oh my, look, there is a staircase!"

Lilly just looked at her not sure what to think. "Can I go to the bathroom now?"

"Yes, go now," Rose said. "Don't anyone look."

When Lilly was finished Rose yelled to the group, "Come here guys, you must see!"

Fitz looked at the others and shook his head and said, "Five minutes, then we proceed back home."

Once they saw what Rose saw all sense of time became lost. In front of them were stairs made into the side of a wall. One wondered, how old they were. Were they still on their property or was this someone else's?

"We have to take a peek," pleaded Emmaline.

"Two people go up and the rest of us will stay here," ordered Fitz.

"Robert and I will take a peek. You wait here; we won't be long," said Emmaline.

"You have five minutes according to the timepiece. Start now," Fitz said.

Quickly and without reservation the pair ascended the stairs made of dirt and old stones spilled over with greenery. They didn't fall but used their hands to assist them. The wall was twice their height and once at the top they were careful not to step by the edge. They walked around for a moment and could see they were indeed somewhere which belonged to someone else. The pair walked over to a small wooden structure with no windows. It had a door. And beyond that they saw water. It was a pool, an outdoor pool.

"They won't believe this, even if we tell them," said Robert.

Emmaline shook her head in agreement. They discovered a private pool out here in the mountains near their lake. "We'll have to ask my father about this. He must know his neighbors," she said, not so sure. "But if we do tell the others, then our parents will know and we might not be allowed to come here anymore."

"How can you know your neighbors miles and miles away?" he asked with big round eyes.

"Right, let's not disturb anything. Off we go. Should we tell the others or let it be our secret?" she asked.

"Emmaline, do you want to keep it a secret?" he asked and looked her over.

"I don't know. But if everybody knows, then it will be too noisy and we could never sneak here and go swimming," she said.

"You have a point. I have to think about that," replied Robert, trying to be older than he was. "I'll see what I can find out about the neighbors, miles and miles away, from my dad or yours when we review the maps again. I just won't let on what we have seen."

"Let's go. We can talk about it tomorrow," she said. She rather liked having a secret only they knew about.

Carefully they retreated down the stairs where the others were waiting with big eyes.

"What did you find?" asked Lilly.

"More forest and mountains that must belong to the neighbors," he replied in a lackluster tone.

"Lots of territory in the Carolinas with mountains, rivers and forests, that's for sure!"

The group got back in hiking formation and found the creek. Not another word was spoken until dinner time. They indeed made it back in time, which the parents acknowledged, and gave them their respect and admiration. The parents especially liked the idea of a swim test. Good thinking they told the kids. They would probably get to go back for sure. Robert told his dad he wanted to review the large map of the place so he could see the surrounding area.

"Sure Robert. We can review that tomorrow," said his father.

"You can even help to improve the map thereby

then I can make more at the press for everyone," said Charles.

Emma and Robert decided to keep the pool to themselves with no clear reason, only uncertainty, in that it made it special. That specialness forged the beginning of a bond for these two souls in the Carolina Mountains. Who knows why these things happen? Maybe its birth order, or knowledge or possibly being a middle child with an only child friend suited their needs. One thing was for certain and Robert knew this, even at the age of eleven, Emma was an adventurer like himself and he needed someone by his side if he was to set out into the world of discovery.

Garrett, the chef or cook, set out for the town of Boone to purchase supplies. Deuce, the horseman was the driver. Mr. Johnson warned the two of them that they were in the south and to be careful. Deuce knew exactly what he meant as not everybody he learned accepted the fact the south lost the war to the union. Obtaining supplies in the sleepy little town of Boone should be just fine, as they'd stopped their previous to the arrival at the summer homes. He warned them, no other stops. Be quick and leave, just in case.

Garrett retrieved the list he'd made once in town at the Boone General Store which was a feed and supply store that catered to the local folks. Lately, though, the owner had a few northerners with mountain property in need of general supplies for the summer. He recognized Garrett from last week. How could one not remember the jet black hair with blue eyes that danced around in a lively way? Also, his thick accent gave him away and one had to ask him to repeat himself twice or more.

After Garret had repeated himself three times, he exclaimed, "Oh my here's the list!"

"Hey, Garrett, I understood that. You'll just have to slow down, then I can catch on. You hear?" asked the owner.

"Mr. Smith, yes I will, next time. Here ye go!" Garrett handed him the list and then left the counter to obtain a couple of personal items. Deuce had waited outside in the car trying to be a bit inconspicuous.

"Mr. Johnson has some mighty fine looking cars, quite a few of them, huh?" asked the store owner.

"Yes, he has four to be certain," replied Garrett.

"How nice. They didn't give you a problem with the long drive from the north?" he asked.

"Not really, just two blown tires we repaired with a couple spares. It took a week and a half, that was the hard part getting in and out of rooms and on our way," alliterated Garrett, slowly and smoothly.

The bell gave a light ring when the front door opened and it was Deuce. He acknowledged the store owner and Garrett. "We'll need to order and purchase something to eat for the trip back up the mountain," said Deuce.

"You are absolutely right!" said Garrett.

The store owner said, "My name is Jesse and let me know if there is anything else you boys need. I want to be sure Mr. Johnson and his family have all the comforts just like up north." He smiled at the two of them. They returned the cordial greeting.

"Thank you, I'm Deuce and you've met Garrett, though, you might have not understood him," said Deuce. They all laughed. The pair loaded up the supplies, paid and then were on their way out the front door. Jesse had given them some spicy beef, almost like a thick stew and homemade bread enclosed in brown waxed paper. He poured them a root beer or sarsaparilla his wife maid, and told them they could eat their meal right out front at one of the tables he had on the porch. And so they did.

Deuce and Garrett talked on the way home about the supplies and how things were going. They both liked it here, each wondered about possibly staying on but were unsure about the winter. They needed to approach Mr. Johnson and discuss this possibility. Certainly, DJ and Elizabeth would return to the north but there was also Francis, the gardener. Francis had told Deuce he'd like to stay. The guys decided they needed to talk with Mr. Johnson. They wouldn't have to wait for when they returned Mr. Johnson held a family council meeting and invited their friends the neighbors, Charles and Mary Stephens.

Right before dinner was served at the Johnson's in the oversized dining room, which one end looked out over the valley and the other end up to the mountains above, Mr. Johnson held a meeting.

Ruth began. She asked everyone to sit at the table in their respective places. She had the girls make place settings and place cards with their names. There were a few moments of scattered confusion. The summer house was not decorated yet, only furniture filled the place. Next year she planned to do just that.

"Mrs. Stephens and I plan to decorate the summer houses next year so your input is encouraged as to your favorite colors, etc. The plaid curtains are the exception in Mary's house."

"Really mother? You'll let us decide," Rose said.

"Absolutely. This is to be a place for calmness and serenity, a place to escape to and feel like one is on a holiday for rest. You don't even have to read the newspaper if you don't want to know the news, except of course, Mr. Stephens whose business is to know the news." She carried on. DJ came in and poured the adults wine, the children received Pearls lemonade.

Little did the family know that this summer and these few special moments in the dining room would change for Mr. Johnson who dealt in spirits and wine? His world and that of his family along with these summers would become precarious and dry when Prohibition began in January 1920, but that was six months away.

For now the families enjoyed North Carolina and their mountain summer homes. Extensive plans were made by the adults while the children looked for adventure and play, horseback riding included. Emmaline and Robert managed to go to their special place and swim together in the secret pool as often as they could. They made sure no one was looking and never told the others. They had no idea who it belonged to and they never saw anyone swimming. They had found a little place all their own. How they managed to keep the secret forever was almost beyond themselves. But at the end of the summer in 1921 there was a drastic change and all the bliss and consummate living in the mountains would cease with the candor spoken by Jack Johnson. The days of yore had reached their fermentation and the young lives would woefully claim turbid days like the river after a mighty storm.

Mr. Johnson made a declaration in the dining room. "We will not be coming here next summer. I am moving our family to Chicago, due to business," he stammered out for all to hear at dinner.

Gasps and stares at the family man who had endeared their hearts and helped to prosper fortunes became direct and succinct. They were all tethered to this man and they watched as the once loving, larger than life man, became surly and downtrodden in the way he spoke. It was as though the life had left Mr. Johnson. The ephemeral etiquette belied his true character and he was going to relieve them of a recent tradition they had come to love ... summer's in North Carolina. But what could they do?

Robert looked at Emmaline across the table. He could tell she had no idea of this news. They had so much uncharted territory to still explore. Much to the chagrin of Robert his own father declared they too might possibly take a summer off since they would miss the Johnson's. What? Fitz turned askance and began sobbing. He didn't know what else to do. This decision made him sad. He stood up at the table without permission.

"Father, we can come and you can move to Chicago!" he shouted.

"Fitz, the family stays together and Chicago is too far for summer's here. We don't have to sell and maybe, later, we'll come back. There are trains, but for now we'll miss a few summer's. Final, that's a done deal," Jack Johnson said sternly.

No one wanted dessert. The succulent peaches were returned to the kitchen and Garrett himself, rather sad and despondent, decided to cook pies. He knew the families and the times they'd cherished would be remembered fondly in the morning after they retreated and let the bad news sink in for a while. Everyone would be ready for dessert then. He made a cream topping and stored it in the cellar for the morning.

Mr. Johnson announced that he was hiring a local farm hand to check on the place during the winter. The horses would be sold. All of his employees would be moving with the family. After they were settled, then possibly a few could return here to keep the place during the summer. He'd have to see when the time is right.

"Let's saddle up the horses and take them for a ride," said Deuce. He could see the long, sad faces that needed some cheer. Mr. Johnson acknowledged the kind idea with a nod of his head.

Perfect idea he thought. Three great years and now he had a business and a house to sell up north. His business had been shut down by June of this year, 1921, two years after the Act of Prohibition. There were so many things he could not tell his family. The family business that had been in his name and his grandfather's was in peril and he thought he was doing the right thing. Only time would tell. He would carry this burden by himself and not detail his family on the specifics.

Chapter 3

This was likely the easiest travel for the five of them but the longest move they had ever made, especially by train. The servants: from Garrett, the Irish chef; Deuce, the Southern horseman with African American roots; Francis, the French gardener; DJ, the English/Canadian butler; Elizabeth, the English nanny and even their pets, Petals and London, were all in the automobiles, model 'T's', and headed to Chicago. The family would see them within a week.

Ruth and Jack Johnson departed from the train first, followed by Rose and Fitz, and finally, Emmaline, who held Lilly's hand as they carefully descended the steps. Here they were in a new town in Ohio for a whole week. The kids looked around for their next adventure, especially Fitz, but it looked like all the towns they had just passed from New York to Cleveland.

"Don't worry Fitz," said his dad, "the lake is a mere mile or two away."

"Yes, sir," he replied.

"Let's get our luggage and cross the street. There's the hotel, that brick structure more than a few stories tall with a hitching post out front and automobiles parked on the street," said Mr. Johnson. He was glad to be off the train and halfway to his new home in Chicago. He'd had to sell his business and go to work for others after prohibition dried up his factories. His bank went in the red and now, his livelihood, belonged to someone else he'd never met. He was to have a meeting with several men here and then be employed in Chicago. He'd been assured of a salary due to the nature of his previous experience with spirits and such, winemaking, too. His wife did not know how dire the circumstances had become. He almost had to sell off the Carolina property, but saved that until the end. The sale of his home, businesses in New York was more valuable than he'd realized, so for now things were looking good. Even this small vacation was a real treat, the extra money from the sale of his home more than covered his travel expenses and fun for the family.

The Johnson's checked in while the children waited outside on the front porch. Once the transaction was complete they were shown to their rooms on the third floor. Ruth opened her door and began to settle in when she heard loud voices.

"Flowers! Who are they from? Who are they for?' exclaimed Lilly. Emmaline and Rose ran to the table and searched for a card. Lilly followed them. "Looking for this?"

"Give it to me, Lilly!" demanded Rose.

"Here, Emmaline, you read it," she instructed. Lilly smirked at her older sister Rose.

Ruth walked in to see the three young girls surrounding the large bouquet of cut flowers. They were beautiful with roses, carnations and zinnias, even a magnificent sunflower in the middle beaming bright yellow hues.

She looked at Emmaline and waited for her to read the note.

"My dear friends Fitz, Rose, Lilly and Emmaline-I wish you all the best on your trip to Chicago. What an adventure! I wish I was going. Maybe someday I can come and visit. My mother let me send you flowers; she said there's a first time for everything. Thanks for being friends. I'll miss you, Robert."

Rose and Emmaline hugged with Lilly right in the middle. "That's so sweet. What a nice boy!" said Ruth. She left the room before she cried.

All the arrangements were made with a trolley ride to downtown Sandusky and then they would board a steamer boat over to Cedar Point, followed by walking the park and visiting all the sights and rides. Yes, an adventure was to be had. Jack bought two days' worth of fun and the other two days he'd have meetings. The kids could play games or read at the hotel.

Jack Johnson took his meeting with two men he had never met before. They had a couple addresses written out for him to keep. "Look these up when you get into town, the owner will be waiting for you. He expects you to see him next Tuesday, which will give you a couple days to get settled. He likes your experience and expects you will do well. Fairly soon the Act will be overturned and it will be business as usual," one of the men said.

He didn't believe them about the Act and he wasn't sure exactly what he would be doing, but he needed the money, so he took the job. Chicago was a new frontier on the water with lots of opportunities, he was told.

Jack took the notes and agreed to meet his new boss on Tuesday in Chicago.

The men toasted and saluted to Jack and his new job. Fitz looked over at his dad through the breezeway between the two rooms. He didn't like the looks of the men his dad was having a drink with but what did he know. They didn't look like his usual customers in New York. He had gone on delivery runs with his dad and these two didn't fit the part. He shrugged it off, they were going to Cedar Point tomorrow for the whole day. He might even get to see a real lion and his dad promised him he could try the skeet shoot, whatever that was. He would be doing it with his dad and that would be mighty fine indeed. Fitz smiled at this thought.

On the third day they went to Cedar Point for the second time. Everyone wore smiles in anticipation. They knew what they were in for! The trolley glided over the streets barely missing the motorists and carriages. Chaos is what Rose thought, then she saw the water. "Look ahead, there's the boat coming into dock right now. I think it's ours," she exclaimed.

Lilly missed her dog Petals whenever she saw another dog. This made her a bit homesick and then when she thought about home, she wanted to cry. She didn't have a home, not yet. Then she thought about Cedar Point and the Leap Frog Railway. She couldn't wait to ride it again. New York left her mind.

What is it about going high up the sky and riding on a train that seemed to be sailing? The family stood in line and waited their turn for The Leap Frog Railway. There was plenty of people in the park but so many different things to do that it didn't seem crowded. Once up in the sky, traveling around, they forgot their cares and worries of the day. They cooled off under some trees with a lemonade.

"I want to go swimming!" shouted Emmaline.

"I do too!" exclaimed her sisters in unison.

"I want to but when are we going skeet shooting, dad?" asked Fitz.

"Settled, Fitz and dad go shooting and we four ladies will go swimming," said their mother.

"As soon as we are ready I know where the bath house is mother," said Emmaline.

Once inside the bath house the ladies began to undress and put on the rented garments. Only their lower legs and ankles were exposed, in addition to some arms and necks. They were given caps but declined to put them on. They wanted to feel the water on their head. They strolled a short ways on the boardwalk where other ladies had strollers or buggy carts which they pedaled. Once they found the gate, they entered and walked on the sand. It was hot!

They ran to the water's edge and put their feet in the cool Lake Erie water.

"Oh, this is so much better," Rose said softly with relief.

"Can you swim mother?" asked Lilly.

"Yes, as a matter of fact I can. I learned how to

in a small lake in New York. Both my parents could swim and they taught me," said Ruth.

She and Emmaline walked out until the water covered their shoulders. "Come in you two," said Emmaline.

Lilly ran into the water, splashing and making as many waves as she could. She was used to the lake as she had swam in North Carolina every summer for three years.

The ladies stayed in the water most of the day, occasionally coming out and going to sit upon their blankets. The day was beautiful, the day was still, was it really real or my mind confused by will? Rose began thinking of poetry and wished to recite her mother's favorite poems. "May I mother?"

"I would love to hear it; have you rehearsed it and know it by heart?" Ruth asked her daughter.

"I know it. I do," said Rose.

Dreams *by Edgar Allan Poe*
Oh! That my young life were a lasting dream!
My spirit not awak`ning till the beam.

A Dream Within a Dream *by Edgar Allan Poe*
Take this kiss upon the brow!
And, in parting from you now.
Thus much let me avow--

You are not wrong, who deem;
Yet if Hope has flown away
In a night, or in a day,
In a vision, or in none,
Is it therefore the less gone?
All that we see or seem
Is but a dream within a dream.

I stand amid the roar
Of a surf tormented shore,
And I hold within my hand
Grains of the golden sand--
How few! Yet how they creep
Through my fingers to the deep
While I weep--while I weep!
O God! Can I not grasp
Them with a tighter clasp?
O God! Can I not save
One from the pitiless wave?
Is all that we see or seem
But a dream within a dream?

They all clapped for Rose. "Beautiful Rose, just beautiful. You are going to be on stage. I just know it," exclaimed her mother.

"I know what I'm gonna do mother," said Lilly, catching them all by surprise.

"Tell us Lilly. Tell us, right now," said Emmaline.

Just as Lilly began swinging her arms forward and backwards opposite each other, she moved her legs and feet the opposite also and then she sang, "Charleston, Charleston, just wanna do the Charleston."

"Lillian Georgina Johnson, stop that! You are in public, stop that!" warned mother as she looked around. Then when she stopped, amazed at her mother's request, she thought to laugh aloud. They all joined her in laughter.

"I'm going to be a Jazz singer, in a club, just like the ones in New York City!" exclaimed Lilly.

Lilly looked at her mother with big round eyes pleading for her to say yes. Yes, honey, do it. But that didn't come, not from Ruth's era. Nope.

"I'll come see you at the clubs when I'm old enough. I can't wait, "Emmaline told her.

"What are you going to be Emmaline?" asked Lilly.

"I don't know. Not yet, anyway. Maybe, I'll be a tennis player, a traveler or maybe a seamstress, but most likely a mother," replied Emmaline. "Eventually, I want to have babies."

"Where will you travel Emmaline?" asked Rose. She wanted to know this.

"I suppose south to Florida. I'd like to see the

palm trees and feel the hot sun, maybe even eat a fresh pineapple or coconut off the tree."

Rose looked at her quizzically. "I suppose you want to go traveling with a pirate, too."

"Something like that. I don't know. I just want to see the world and not stay put. I want to keep going, searching for new things. It's in my blood or something," said Emmaline. "Ask mother, maybe she knows why."

The girls looked at mother but there was a strange moment of silence and no one knew why. Ruth pretended she didn't hear that last comment.

"Let me read you a few lines from a magazine, a jazz magazine at that."

"'Woman goes from an extension of man, from virtues like pleasing, obedience, self-sacrifice, beauty, fidelity, tenderness and affection, which were gratifying to men. We called her our better half, a chivalrous remark but really we regarded her as inferior and kept her in subordination.'"

Ruth continued on...

"'Her body belonged to the husband, her mind to her home and her heart to her children,'" said Ruth. Vanity Fair was the name of the magazine mother held in her hands as she read to us.

The girls looked at her with puzzled expressions. None of them knew what to say. Then the eldest changed the subject.

"I'll get to vote in the next election, which is after this very next one of 1924. I'll get to choose the president of the United States," declared Rose who was sixteen.

"Someday, I will, too," declared Lilly.

Later that day the Johnson family rode the steamboat Boeckling back to the docks in Sandusky bay, then took the trolley back towards their hotel. They walked several blocks and made it just in time for dinner in the hotel dining room. A telegram was waiting for Mrs. Jack Johnson. It would be read privately later that night.

Jack insisted she keep the note private. "You must keep quiet. You've gone this far, you can go all the way Ruth. It's for the best, for everyone. I assure you."

She shed tears that night which he did not dry for he was the cause of them to begin with, even though he had tried to help. *She'll forget about it in Chicago*, he thought. He hoped. And then he never gave it another thought.

In the morning, Ruth looked at Lilly and the letter crossed her mind. But she must put it away, maybe someday something good might happen, but not now.

The Sandusky Register-Journal headline ran

'Naked Swimmers Seized by Police at Point.' Jack lay the paper on the breakfast table where his family had gathered in the Murschel House on North Depot Street in Sandusky, Ohio. Emmaline's eyes about popped out of their sockets.

"What?"

"It's a good thing you ladies weren't swimming last night when they caught some youth swimming naked, no clothes, no suits or coverage," Jack said. He chuckled and couldn't imagine how they took them in to jail.

"I want to do that!" shouted Emmaline.

"Of course you do, Emma," said Fitz. He shook his head.

The next day the family boarded the train on North Depot Street in July of 1922 bound for Chicago. Their idyllic life would never be the same but they didn't know this as a photographer took the family photo in front of the train station. Jack Johnson paid for this image showcasing his family.

Chapter 4

"All aboard," shouted the engineer. The passengers were on board and had found their seats.

The Johnson family practically took up a whole car. This passenger train was headed to Chicago, with a few stops and a time change or two, it would be there by midnight. Their train accommodations consisted of two sleeper rooms and a small dining area with two love seats facing each other and the six seats next to the windows two by two. *Very nice* thought Jack. One last hurrah before he settled into this new job. He would not be his own boss, like he was used to. Therefore, he justified these expenses.

The girls, Rose and Lilly, sat together, followed by Fitz at the window with Emmaline and in the third row were the parents, Ruth and Jack. Fitz stared out the window searching for birds or wild animals. The scenery went on and on into nothingness. He did see an occasional flock of geese that seemed to be going from pond to pond, probably in search of food. The railroad went near the lake and then back again into nothing. He saw a home every now and then with fields of corn. It was very tall, possibly taller than himself. He envisioned himself running through these fields maybe chasing Emma or Lilly, or playing hide and seek. One could get lost all day he supposed.

They went past several small cities and somewhere just inside Indiana he fell asleep. The girls went and lay down in their sleeper car while Ruth and Jack talked business. They discussed schools, the property and house, and the servants that were meeting them there. Jack assured her the house would be plenty large in size with comforts of electric power for light. Outside light would use gas but indoors would have switches to turn on and off. They both seemed pleased at the thought of their new city and home.

"Mother, I thought you said Chicago was like New York, big and all with lots of buildings," said Lilly.

"Oh, yes Lilly that is what I've been told. Out here you are just seeing the vast horizons of America as it has pushed west all the way to the Pacific Ocean. Tonight we will see the city with lights on before we arrive at the station. Then there will be many cars, trolleys, horses and carriages with lots of people," she assured her youngest daughter.

"Hope so, because I wouldn't want to live out here where there are no people!" exclaimed Rose.

Dinner was served at eight on the train and the group was told that the train would arrive before eleven into the station. Fitz thought he rather liked this train travel with everything right here. He could look out the window, eat dinner and go take a nap while traveling. It seemed rather comfortable he thought. His mind wandered to what a boat or large steamship might be like. He'd never crossed the ocean, yet. Maybe he should do that someday. He started to dream about boats with sails and motors, even little row boats. Fitz with his naps passed the time on the train and before he knew it he heard a whistle blow loudly and the passenger car he resided in slowed down. They were entering the station.

It only took a few days before they began settling in their newly purchased large Victorian home on the lake. Two nights were spent at the Drake Hotel, one of Chicago's finest. His new boss paid for this as he met him for meetings during the day. Mrs. Ruth Johnson had daily tea in the Fountain Court, while the girls explored this grand hotel near the lake.

Soon they would start a new life in this city on Lake Michigan. Right off their backyard was the beautiful lake. It surprised them every morning with a sunrise before they set off for school. It waited for them to return and then they would bring Petals down to the shore. They tried and succeeded only once to put London in the water. Relentless attempts with failure made them give it up when one day the cat just seemed to say, "all right already, you win." He shook himself off just a little after sprinting to the water's edge, turned and eyed all of them. Oh to read a cat's mind, thought Fitz.

He sat back on his hind legs and surveyed the area. Then walked slowly to the water and put his tiny mouth in for a drink. He looked up at Fitz and hissed so loud. All of the swimmers decided it wasn't worth it, no more lake for London. He ran back to the house as fast as lightning strikes.

At night the back yards of these fancy homes were lit up with candles, lights and fires. There seemed to be parties several nights a week. Times were lively and lit up at night added by the moon when it reflected off the lake. When the cars arrived in the evenings and Mr. Johnson already planned on replacing one of these with a fancier model. His boss was paying him well, for the knowledge he had of the liquor business. They owned him actually. All of this was loaned to him, this big life. He told Ruth nothing of the kind. He carried this inside himself.

How could he tell her otherwise? He had to be the big man. *In time,* he thought, *the Prohibition Act would be repealed.*

The cars were getting longer, more colorful and shinier. While the ladies dresses rose up the leg with a slimming appearance, hats were now sexier, more fitted. Women could vote and drink at these speakeasy clubs and almost all of them smoked. Change was everywhere and moving fast. Lilly and her 'Charleston song and dance routine' were a hit at her parents' parties. She reveled in it. Rose turned seventeen and one would have thought she owned the town. She thought so anyway and had many suitors, the parlor filled on a daily basis it seemed. This delighted her to no end. She wanted to be on stage so she frequented a theatre and enrolled in a class.

Fitz worked on his sports abilities after school and found a job at a local deli store. His dad told him to find something like store ownership or banking and not follow him in his own endeavors, whatever those were now, Fitz had no idea. He didn't even think his mother knew nor wanted to know. Strange, but to Fitz, he thought his Dad told him more than he told his Mother. Maybe she really was in the dark about it all. Maybe his Dad confided in him for a reason.

Lilly took voice and dance lessons and performed at every opportunity available. She developed confidence and bravado, her mother called it. She also began to read the papers and wanted to perform at places but wasn't sure about the age category. Approaching the age of twelve, she needed to be sixteen to sing at clubs. She pursued Rose to help her to look older out of the site of her own mother.

Ruth enjoyed her family, prepared for the frequent parties and generally enjoyed life. She'd forgotten about that letter and what was left behind. Occasionally, she heard from Mary in New York. Mary told her that Pearl left for Florida to work down there with a relative. She was sad to see her go but knew she wanted to be near family. Robert was doing fine. He was sixteen and would be going to college soon. He was extremely smart, didn't really need to study because he was so interested in everything. She supposed he got that from his father. She said maybe one day she'd ride the train and come visit her. She didn't know when.

Chapter 5

The autumn was a busy time settling in the new Victorian home on Lake Michigan. The avenue was rather stately with several families moving in at the same time. Quickly, they began to familiarize themselves with small parties that grew into larger affairs as their status grew in the city of Chicago. Mrs. Johnson stayed busy just keeping up with her family, either sewing or buying new clothes for her girls, boy, and husband, too.

Something they were used to was cold winters but they would experience the lake effect friends kept telling them. "What is the lake effect?" asked Lilly.

"Lilly, my dear, my associates tell me children love it but businesses quiet down and our automobiles cannot be driven very far, or at all," Jack Johnson replied.

"That means no school!" she shouted.

Her father looked at her and smiled at her delight. He liked the idea she was full of spirit as he had surely lost his. Certain things he kept from his family; they didn't need to know the fast pace of the liquor business and how lucrative it had become. He had decided after reaching Chicago and realizing his true measurement of work there that he would do this for a few years and move to his summer home in Carolina and become a farmer, maybe grow a crop. But for now the place was on fire with so many joints and speakeasies needing liquor. The desire for his product had reached a need he could hardly serve. Too bad his son wasn't old enough, he thought, then quickly dismissed that idea. The Johnson's had never been above the law and he wouldn't let any of them follow him. He didn't tell them he was doing illegal business and they didn't ask.

"Jack, I'll need an evergreen to decorate for Christmas," Ruth said as she walked in the room where Lilly and Jack were talking.

He looked startled, a million miles away, but instantly drew himself back to his wife.

"Let's make it a family affair. I know a place not far from here to chop a tree down. Someone gave me a tip yesterday."

"Friday after school we can do that. I'm going to have a party after our tree is decorated and invite many of our friends. The girls and I will go shopping for some ornaments and we can make some, too. Lilly, will you help me make cookies for the party?"

"Yes, ma'am!" Lilly said with delight. "Can we make extra to eat before the party?"

"I'm sure we'll have to test them before we share them," said Ruth.

"What about Rose and Emma?" Lilly inquired.

"Rose has been asked to attend a special dance and Emma wants to help her pick out a dress, so they will be busy. It's you and I; we'll let them frost the cookies with icing later on."

"Mother, I want to sing a song at our party. Can I?"

"Yes, you can. But you must rehearse it for me first. Deal?"

"Deal."

The family picked out a tree for Christmas. Actually, Jack stopped along the road and he and Fitz went into the woods and chopped one down, figuring the size and what might fit in their large great room that faced the lake. They both agreed mother would like it and she did.

When the family awoke on Saturday morning Lilly informed them they'd had their first snowfall. As soon as she said it each one looked out the window, indeed a light dusting had covered the ground with about a half inch of white powder.

"Predictions are for half a foot of snow," said Jack Johnson.

His family looked at him and Rose asked, "How do you know that, father?"

"Someone told me that yesterday who has lived here their whole life. He can tell by the wind and skies, the color of the skies that is. Everyone who knows him said you can trust him, he knows what he is saying. He's right most of the time," said Jack.

"That and telegrams from the west I learned in school. The west gets our weather first, out there in the mountains, so we can expect it a few days later, most of the time!" Emma reported gleefully. She was studying geography, electricity and inventions in school.

"Are you studying your favorite subject, yet?" asked her father.

"Not yet, in the spring we will the teacher informed me," she replied.

"Sorry you have to wait so long, especially with the cold winter. There will be ice everywhere, I'm told."

"I can't wait. I'm going to take up a sport in the spring, too."

"What's that Miss Emma?"

"Tennis!"

"Tennis. Then you will be moving south someday to play tennis and study plants, I suppose," he uttered.

"Yes, I will enjoy the winters for now and play in the snow with Lilly because someday I won't live here," said Emma. She spoke it like she was a gypsy who knew her fortune. *Maybe she did,* he thought.

Emma and Rose walked a few blocks and visited several stores to purchase Christmas tree ornaments, a dress and, of course, sweets from a sweet shop. Mother and Lilly stayed home and baked cookies, beginning in the morning and endlessly into the afternoon, and finally ending in the early evening. Jack and Fitz went to a local delicatessen where Fitz would be working. Mr. Johnson wanted this for his son, to be employed by an honest hard working fellow. Fitz would learn how to make an honest wage even before he went to college, if that was in his future.

In the Christmas shop Emma found some stationery she absolutely adored and decided to purchase it. A lady with a wreath-like floral expression which circled around her head wrapped in a long flowing sleeveless sinewy gown greeted her from the piece of paper. She was looking at fireflies on the water. Her first letter would be to Robert in New York. She had not forgotten about the flowers he had sent the family when they arrived in Sandusky, Ohio after their departure from the great New York City on their train trip move to Chicago. She had been thinking about him lately and missed their time together down south at the summer homes their families owned side by side.

Rose couldn't wait to show Mother the dress when she got home. The mother-daughter duo were still baking so Rose ran upstairs to try on the dress and show it off. Emma went in the kitchen and promptly helped herself to a cookie and before biting into it she asked.

"May I?"

"Have two Emma! Tell me which is your favorite the sugar or the gingerbread?" directed Lilly.

She looked at her dear little sister and wondered how on earth she got so excited over cookies. Emma shook her head. "I shall have to have more help deciding this most important feat." She grabbed four cookies, two of each and darted off for the staircase. She knew exactly who she'd ask to help her.

Emma sat at her desk and drew up a letter to her old childhood friend Robert. She sat there in a dreamy state for quite a while tasting her two cookies. She found a small box and wrapped the two other cookies up in the very tissue paper from the store. Then she stuffed them in the stationery box and wrapped it again in more paper. Quickly, she devised a letter, familial in nature. She was only twelve and didn't entertain thoughts like Rose did. Rose told her today when she tried the pretty dress on she was going to kiss her man again. Emma's faced showed her the shock she elicited.

"Don't fret Emma. Someday, you too will want to kiss your man, or guy. You will dream about it, trust me." Emma was reliving her older sister's words, over and over. Who she would kiss she wondered. She continued on with the letter and never in her mind did she give Robert a thought about kissing him. It just didn't even enter her brain.

Dear Robert,

I heard you are doing rather extraordinary in school. I knew you were extremely smart, that's why you and I get along so well. We don't fret over such insignificant items. Instead we look beyond what is in front of us, except in the case of a small dare.

Don't you miss swimming in our secret pool? We were invariably lucky to have gotten away with that for three summers. The others never even suspected anything. I dubiously enjoy that they don't know anything about our pleasure. Maybe we should invite them next time we summer there.

Lilly has helped mother to bake Christmas

cookies and you get the benefit. I'm sending you two of her creations but you must decide which the better cookie is. Write me and let me know. I don't know how long mail takes to reach New York. That is something I should know. I bet you do.

Merry Christmas Robert to you and your family. That's me on the cover of the letter. Do you like it? I'm not sure where I am but I look very mysterious and full of joy.

Probably, I am on a journey with you somewhere in the tropics!

Sincerely,
Emmaline

Chapter 6

The Christmas party had been planned, the large Victorian home decorated and more snow had been added to the grounds outside. The lake was like glass with no movement. It was Friday night and Rose had promised two people favors for the night. Her date was coming by to take her out for the evening. Her date was beyond her years, but she lied to her mother as she wanted badly to be with this new beau. The other person was her youngest sister Lilly. Why she promised her what she did she would never know. But somehow she just couldn't say no when she asked. Lilly had read about a club, an out of the way place and it happened that Rose's boyfriend knew of the place. So Rose dressed Lilly in her own frocks but well covered up and did her hair and makeup and snuck her out the back door while mother was upstairs. Father was out for the night. Rose's insides were a bit strewn but she decided that it wouldn't hurt anyone and Lilly was good. Lilly sang her a song out in the garage the other day that clinched the deal. Lilly said, "Thanks to Rose, my big sister who helped me get here." Then she bowed to the crowd.

Rose's boyfriend knew the big man at the entrance and they were immediately let in. Lilly was the second act of four on Friday night. After her performance the couple would silently return her to the home on the lake. Rose herself was underage. What were they doing? She laughed. She couldn't help herself, then she turned and kissed her older boyfriend. Rose and he sat in the back of the darkly lit joint. The place was full with only a couple tables left. Her boyfriend Frank bought them a couple drinks and they settled in ready for the first act. The couple didn't really pay much attention and only gave the stage a second look when the applause started. Next up was her sister Lilly.

The announcer hit the stage and thanked the crowd for noticing what a fine singer the gentlemen who just left the stage was indeed. "I have a newcomer, in fact, the next two acts will be performing for the first time. Please welcome Lilac Rain, or as she just told me 'Lilac in the Rain' performing (It Had to Be You) Only You and Charleston!"

Rose didn't stop looking at her sister for one

moment. She was full of pride, even if she had snuck her in here. She decided mother would be proud but she wouldn't admit it. So it was Rose's duty to help the younger Johnson sister, all ten years of her. As soon as she finished though, and before she was behind the curtain, Rose and Frank skinied quickly to the dressing room and retrieved Lilly, rather Lilac. When the new performer answered the door, her eyes lifted as she could hear the applause still going.

"Sweetie, they are still clapping for you. Hurry, we must exit before being found out. Let's go, now," Rose ushered.

Lilly giggled, "Rose, I was not even nervous. Is that a good sign?"

"Honey, I don't know. But they loved you," Rose whispered and kissed her sister on the cheek. She grabbed her hand and the three of them exited before anyone knew they were gone.

Frank drove a little fast in all the haste and arrived at the Johnson house before mother knew anyone had left. It was only ten thirty and she was busy getting ready for tomorrow's party, her and her help. Lilly ran upstairs to wash off the pancake makeup applied by Rose. Rose only wished she could share what just transpired, but it wasn't proper and she knew it. For now, it was their secret. Except 'Lilac in the Rain' was really good and people like to talk when they discover talent. Rose couldn't hide Lilly forever and that wasn't the plan. Frank told her she needed to be around thirteen and then, maybe, she could audition for more clubs. He'd check around he told Rose. Rose kissed Frank for a long time that night on the front porch. Lilly went to bed with a smile planted on her cheeks and stars in her eyes. She thought for a moment she might have even fainted while lying in bed, then she heard a knock on the door. It was her mother.

"Lilly, dear. Good night sweetie. The big party is tomorrow and I'll need your help. Your father has agreed to let you perform for our guests, too. Is that okay with you? Emma can play the piano for you while you sing," said mother.

"Yes, mother. Sounds lovely. I mean I would love to do that. It will be my first big performance!" And then Lilly was sure she passed out into slumber land forever.

Saturday came and the house was a buzz with a flurry of ladies going this way and that. Lilly and Rose couldn't help themselves and smiled at one another several times over the course of the morning. Lilly helped her mother with arrangements of garland and then table settings for food later that night. The silver needed polishing and she gladly helped to make it shine. Somehow this made her smile even more. Her mother noticed her smiling, grinning, or whatever quite a bit. Doesn't every mother notice the small things with their children?

"Lilly dear, what has you so happy? Is it because Christmas is so close and you enjoy baking with me?" asked Ruth.

Lilly stopped and her eyebrows rose up on her forehead. "Well, mother you see I have finally found what my true self is, what I'm supposed to do with my life." She turned and stared at her mother who didn't know what to make of that.

"Whatever do you mean by that, my dear? You are too young to do anything but help me now and then," replied Ruth.

"Oh, heavens no mother!" retorted Lilly.

And with that Ruth looked at her youngest daughter puzzled and then decided to play along. "I know this is your make believe grown up self. What will you be?"

"It's not what I will be or become mother, it's what I am," Lilly replied, all ten years of her.

Silence.

"I will show you tonight what I can do, you and your guests," Lilly said calmly.

Ruth smiled. She'd taught her daughters fairly well. The times were a changing and they would do what she could not. Oh, to be twenty again for a day or a night. "I simply cannot wait."

Fitz and his father Jack set up an outside area for a fire as the guests could warm up outside when they took a stroll down by the water. Lake Michigan was cold but not frozen over as yet. Typically, they were told, it was January when that occurred. Several lanterns were ready to be lit on a large table outside which further added to the charm of the back yard. Jack told Fitz some guests would probably begin caroling out here in the cold. He'd done that a few times over the years, sing outside this time of year, especially when it snowed. Fitz looked forward to that, he wanted to join in.

An hour or so before the festive party there was a knock at the door. A telegram arrived for Emmaline and her family. It was from Robert in New York. He must have received the cookies she sent him.

"What does it say mother?" she asked.

"Here, it's for you. You read it," said her mother.

"Merry Christmas from our family to yours! The cookies tasted fabulous and I tried to decide which one I liked best and just couldn't. Could you send me more and then maybe I can try the taste test again?" Robert Stephens.

Emmaline laughed. "I'll send him more cookies. And someday, I'll do more than that."

Chapter 7

Jack Johnson walked out his front door and didn't stop until he got in the street. The sun had set and the street lights were lit. Dusk. Snow covered the streets with a light dusting and all was quiet. He guessed people were home getting prepared for an evening out and hadn't hit the street as yet. That is precisely what his family was doing at the moment. He'd brought them all this way and settled into a large fancy home. He knew they couldn't return to New York. He was unsure of his business partners and his best friend here in Chicago had a few warnings for him. They'd had dinner and drinks a couple times and Jack parlayed his feelings and uneasiness about his situation. His friend John told him to continue what he was doing and he'd have an investigator look into some of the dealings. Times were moving so fast now it was hard for the good guys to keep up with the bad. He told him it was best not to cause a stir while he was looking into the situation. After all, John told him, "You do produce an illegal substance."

"How am I supposed to be on the right side of the law when it's been legal before? And will be again." Jack would tell him he'd been making it for years, it's a family business and he would not nor could not stop. Simple. Period.

"Then my dear friend someday you might suffer dire circumstances if they don't make it legal again. Don't forget I warned you." John ushered his fifth sermon to him this year alone.

Jack turned around and saw just how fortunate he and his family were. They definitely had arrived here in Chicago. Nobody was lacking. His house was a miraculous structure that barred no expense and the autos he owned lined the drive out back. Even his office inside had hardwoods lining the wall. He told himself what he had been doing was legal and then they changed the law. Everybody drank it and everyplace sold it. It just happened to be an underground business for the moment. He smiled and comforted himself. Hell, it's Christmas. Get inside and enjoy the God damn party, for Christ's sake!

An hour later guests began arriving with their long winter coats, boots and fancy shoes. The ladies wore dresses below the knees and small caps or hats with plumes on their heads. Lilly noticed all the makeup on the ladies. She ran upstairs and insisted Rose make her up with lots of it. She told her, "Tonight is my real debut Rose. Make me look like I belong on stage. I'll give credit to you. I promise. And when I make it big, you'll be my manager and always do my makeup. Okay?"

"Darling, do you promise?" asked Rose.

"What on earth? Rose, what's wrong?" Lilly noticed a tear in her big sister's eye.

She knew she shouldn't tell her little sister. It was too much information for such a young girl. But she couldn't help it. She wanted Lilly to succeed and just maybe, maybe there was a promising career ahead for her. "I'm going to have a baby," said Rose.

"Rose Johnson, you're not married. How can you?"

"Lilly, promise to keep this secret and I won't tell on you for singing at one of those speakeasy places," she returned.

"Rose, you took me there," she replied.

"I know. I know, but you wanted to do it!"

"I'm going to give them a wonderful show tonight, and yes, I will let you take me to New York as soon as I'm ready," Lilly instructed.

"How will we ever pull this off little sis?" asked

Rose.

"Are you going to get married?" asked Lilly.

"Don't tell anyone but I think he may ask me tonight or on Christmas Eve," Rose said. She had made all the plans. One could not embarrass oneself to the world.

"We both are going to have quite a night!"

"I've set up another show for you to enter. This place has a new group coming called the Creole Jazz, it's a band and the owner said you could sing during their intermissions four nights a week. You're going to make some money Lilly while you get some experience."

Lilly just stared at her sister with glazed eyes and couldn't believe what she had just told her. She reached out and hugged her, "I love you Rose."

Emmaline knocked on the door, "Come on guys the party has started. Momma wants us to serve some food and drinks. Then we can go outside near the bonfire."

They all ran downstairs and obeyed the orders of their dear mother. This was her night to show off the whole place and her skills at being the pretty hostess and mother of them all. The servants extended their politeness and skills also. Deuce parked any cars that hadn't found a spot out front and Garrett, Elizabeth and Francis cooked all day a delicious feast of meat pies, vegetable stews, and fine French desserts. Hot cider brewed on the stove and its light musky cinnamon steeped smell wafted through the rooms with wooden floors. The Christmas tree was decorated and stood in the corner next to a large picture window which highlighted the lake in its stillness. It glistened and definitely beckoned the partygoers for a look.

DJ answered the door and greeted the guests welcoming them to the Johnson's. He was glad they arrived safe and told them to have a lovely evening. All this was followed by a Merry Christmas!

Somewhere around ten thirty Mrs. Jack Johnson decided it was ShowTime. Lily's ShowTime. She instructed her to sing Christmas carols with Emmaline playing the piano.

Many people joined in and the whole place at one point was full of merriment, a memory many of them would take home for the holiday itself.

Emmaline stood up and announced that Lilly was going to sing her mother's favorite carol, all by herself. Emmaline winked at Lilly and the two began O Holy Night written in 1847 by Placide Clappeau, a French poet. A couple that was headed for the dining room for a plate of food turned to see what they thought might be a professional singer that the Johnson's may have hired. For a moment they thought they had heard this lovely voice somewhere. When they saw a little girl they dismissed the very idea.

It wasn't until almost midnight that Lilly would get her big chance. The crowd had thinned to about a third or so of the party revelers and actually the noise of talking, joking and general happiness had increased not decreased with less people. Rose decided now was the time. Perfect.

Rose had put Fitz in charge of putting together three trunks for a makeshift stage for Lilly. She would dance and sing atop these trunks in the largest room of the house. Rose gave Lilly some sheet music which her boyfriend had loaned her. Emmaline studied music in school so this was no problem for her. She spread the sheets across the upright piano and lightly played for a quick study.

DJ and Garrett loaded the serving trays with Mr. Johnson's finest bourbon filled glassware that he had retrieved from his locked case. They offered their guests throughout the house on this festive occasion his best liquor. There was no price on these bottles, some of these he'd had for years. John accepted his glass and walked out back near the house but in view of the bonfire. He missed the first tune of Lilly's house debut repertoire. But he wouldn't miss all of it. For now he sipped his bourbon and watched the fire. He was younger than Jack but had made a friend in his client and had quite enjoyed this evening. John always did things by himself and hadn't settled down as yet. He frequented clubs and rather liked the music now a days with the instruments and singers. It had a certain roar to it and the ladies, well, they were so joyful and full of energy he felt like he was having the time of his life. He probably was indeed. As he stood and smiled at the scene before him, roaring fire and carolers singing tunes about mangers and angels, he didn't know that his future was in the door right behind him and within hours his life would be changed forever.

Lilly and Emmaline began their show, Emmaline in a proper green velvet dress with long ringlets and a large bow in her hair, while Lilly dressed like a showgirl with a white satin flapper dress (pinned hem) fringe laden, and though not strapless but spaghetti style shoulders adorned by a feathered boa plaything. On her head she wore a cap of Rose's that let her pretty large eyes beckon her audience for more whilst the newly cut burgundy colored hair was worn short just escaping the special hat of snow white felt. *What a pretty site* thought their mother. The partygoers at this point didn't much care and were in too jolly of a mood to be spoiled by anything. No one thought Lilly at the age of ten was too young to be singing vaudeville or jazzed up tunes. The party was just getting started. The pair kept playing and when they kept receiving applause well, there was no reason to quit.

Francis the French chef who had made most of the desserts was out front when the young man came for Rose. He quietly went inside and retrieved her as the man wanted to talk with her privately, yes, even in the cold. Rose came quickly when Francis described the young man and she didn't even put a coat on. She closed the front door and went to hug her friend but he kept her at arm's length when he began to speak.

"Rose, I'm so sorry."

Silence.

Inside the singing followed by applause brought no smiles or merriment on the cold front porch.

"Sorry?"

"We have to break it off." The young man swallowed and turned his head. "We just can't date anymore. I must concentrate on my studies."

"I thought tonight was going to be special."

"I did too."

"What then?" Rose became mad with fury and heat rose inside her like a furnace being turned on. She felt her heart ignited by pain in the moment.

"I'm not ready for a family. Please understand.

Please."

She pursed her lips. Her eyes glistened over and he became blurry. Why did she somehow know this would happen? She knew it. Her mother warned her of these impropriety moments of hysterical nonsense in the way the world worked.

"Really?" She stiffened, blinked her eyes and jerked her head higher.

"What? What do you mean?" he asked.

"That's the best you can do?" She stood strong. She had no idea where this strength was coming from. Her eyes wanted to let the waterfall go over the edge but her nerves decided she wouldn't be beat. She couldn't fall and be a mess. There was no time for this.

"So you understand?" he asked. He was crying. He felt bad, just not bad enough. His depth did not go as deep as hers.

"No, I don't understand you. While I have strength for two I don't have the willpower for three. Do you understand?" Where the hell did that come from? She must have learned this from her mother or maybe her father. She took a deep breath and went over to wrap her arms around her boyfriend. She held him and put her head on his shoulders, closed her eyes and one tear fell onto his jacket. That's all he would get of Rose Johnson on this night of nights, Lilly's night.

"I do love you, Rose," he said.

"I know. Go now to your family and Merry Christmas," she said. She turned and went inside.

Once inside John listened intently, like he recognized something familiar. Was it the tune or the voice he wasn't sure?

He looked down and Petals the dog was barking at him. He let the dog out and then closed the door. He walked towards the room with the recognizable voice.

Rose closed the front door and immediately dropped the thoughts from her mind. This was Lilly's night and boy she didn't disappoint. Her voice loomed through the house. Rose smiled. She would see to it her and Lilly pursued the vision they talked about. That was forefront on Rose's thoughts. She was going to make the best of the rest of the night, the rest of her life. Nothing was going to spoil it for either of them. Emmaline would take care of Emmaline, everybody knew that, most especially her mother. Rose hurried through the house to the large back room which overlooked the water and saw such a beautiful sight.

Lilly was doing her dance singing up a storm and languishing on certain notes. At ten she already knew how to draw a crowd and please a crowd. John saw it too.

The applause was loud. Rose ran over to her sister helped her down and told the gatherers it was break time. She thanked them and promised one or two more tunes later on, that's if mother would let her. They all laughed.

John in his pin striped suit, dark swept back hair and grand good looks approached them. He looked between them as he tried to figure out the voice. "Forgive me," he started, "you sound familiar in that I mean your voice is so distinct and wonderful, I tend to think maybe I've heard it before."

"Only if you've been to our house before, Lilly does like to practice quite a lot."

"Emma, I'm thirsty are you?" Lilly asked her partner.

"Let's go find something and check out the bonfire!" Emmaline shouted with glee.

The two practically ran away. John kept looking at Rose and wondered where he had seen her. He wasn't sure. It would probably come to him sooner or later. He hoped soon. He wanted to place her. He actually wanted to spend more time with her, though she was still in school. This was her house, he felt just fine having a conversation with one of his client's daughters.

"Can I help you to find something to eat? Are

you hungry or thirsty? You do look a bit pale," he said.

"How kind of you and yes, I am rather hungry as I've taken so much time to get Lilly ready for the party and her debut, I have forgotten myself," Rose said.

"Good, let's go make a couple plates of food and drink," he said. "Do you want to eat outside near the fire? I believe Fitz has been managing the fire all night. He and his friends."

"No, I have a better idea."

Rose held the plates while John loaded the food upon them. Then he retreated to the kitchen and poured himself a fine bourbon and a hot mulled cinnamon cranberry drink for Rose. She was waiting at the bottom of the staircase in the front hall.

"John, come here," she instructed.

He followed her and they went up the stairs, not to sneak off or anything, but to have a moment of quietness. She led them to her room and once inside closed the door. They sat on her small velvet sofa near the front window. They could see the white snow laden street below. Rose felt like she was a million miles away until he brought her back to reality.

"You and Lilly performed out of town a couple of weeks ago, correct?"

She cocked her head and lifted her chin, pausing momentarily in response to his question. "Yes, we did."

"She's awesome and you both know it," he responded. "But your mother and father don't know it. Do they?"

"No they don't. They do think she sings great." Rose didn't know where this was going but for some reason she felt comfort from this man she knew slightly as her father's lawyer. *He was a man to be trusted* she thought.

He ate his food and looked out the window. He seemed lost in thought. He was. He had this beautiful girl sitting next to him, relaxed, and here he was trying to figure out how to get her out of a jam of sorts. "Lilly," he said quietly. "Lilly needs to go to New York and give the big time a try after she gets a couple months experience here in Chicago," he said matter-of-factly.

"Thanks. You're right you know. Thanks for believing." Rose sighed and her whole body relaxed. She smiled and looked out at the snow. Maybe she was dreaming, maybe the angels were fulfilling a plan. Rose saw that half of the plan was laid out, this made her happy. All that was left was her and the baby. She wouldn't burden John with this now, things would work out. She felt it.

Over the next three weeks the Johnson's had Christmas and rang in the New Year. Fitz got his wish of ice skating on the lake in early January. Lilly performed five days a week during the holidays and her mother entered her in a singing contest, which she won. She won a hundred dollars and gave half to the local hospital charity. She kept the other half for a train ticket. She planned to go to New York City when she was old enough she told her father.

One night in mid-January Jack Johnson met with his attorney. He had received a letter from John stating of his transfer to another firm in New York. He had important matters to discuss with him. This was serious business.

"John when are you leaving for New York?'

"Soon, but I must ask you something first," replied John. "I request your permission to take your daughters with me, both Lilly and Rose."

Jack Johnson coughed and about fell out of his chair, but he did not smile. He was serious.

"I know that sounds almost ridiculous. However, Lilly wants to audition and Rose and I could supervise and be her chaperones. I know many people who could help her with a singing career. It's very big now with the ladies. They are able to make a living, quite a good one at that. Lilly is very young but with more training and stage experience, you know it is what she wants. In a couple years," continued John.

Jack cut him off. "No, I mean let me think about Lilly. It's Rose," said Jack when John cut him off.

"Jack, I want to marry your daughter. I know she is young but we could manage. She tells me she loves me. We could wait a year or two if you'd want us to."

"What does Rose want?"

"We have fallen in love. I never expected it to happen, let alone your daughter. We met and talked at your Christmas party and now we want to get married."

"I know sometimes love happens that way. It really does," said Jack. Neither Jack nor Ruth Johnson knew about Rose's baby. Rose assured her parents she was fine and had fallen in love with John. The two of them had big plans which included Lilly.

"I will take good care of them, both of them. Lilly has a future on the stage; we both know that."

Jack looked at John. "I'm pleased. I know you. You are a good man. They will be so lucky to have you by their side."

Seven years later...

One day Fitz and his Dad were walking along the backyard walk by the lake, one of Fitz's favorite places when he told him, "If something happens to me, take care of the family. I'm going to give you the name of my attorney. Visit him and he'll set you up. You'll be able to start your own business and be removed from the liquor sales, unless of course it becomes legal. You understand?"

"No, not really, but I'll do as you say Dad."

"Don't worry, he'll tell you what to do. Promise me you'll visit him two weeks after I'm gone."

Fitz shook his head and his eyes watered. His Dad was scaring him. His boss was going to kill him he suspected. Fitz searched his father's eyes but saw no relief. In fact, he saw nothing. He wasn't there. Then he knew.

"I can do it. I will."

"Act as if you really miss me. Be in mourning and assist your Mother. The girls will cry and you will be the strong one to help carry on. Two weeks after I'm gone."

"Two weeks. When is this going to happen?"

"Valentine's Day. Two months from now on Valentine's Day."

Chapter 8

It was Valentine's Day February 14th, 1929 and Deuce got a call to pick up Mr. Johnson late in the day. His car was in the shop. The paperboy was waving the late edition at the street corner. Deuce had some time to spare so he called out for a copy. The paperboy came over and tossed one in the passenger side of the auto then collected his payment. He went about his way calling out "Extra Extra. Get it right here. Massacre in Chicago!" He looked over and saw the headlines about a massacre. The picture showed strewn bodies which lay across the front page; then he read the headlines. That's when he stepped on the gas and sped up. It couldn't be the same garage. He hoped not. He liked his boss. He'd been good to him his whole life. He was never going anywhere, not ever. It seemed like an hour, an eternity to go eight miles. But he finally made it. He parked and ran into the garage. He didn't see anyone around. No one was here. He looked everywhere. He heard a grunt and a groan.

"Over here, Deuce. I'm over here," said the voice.

He looked in the direction of the voice and followed it behind an auto. Mr. Johnson lay there with his hand over his leg and the other holding his shoulder.

"You okay? You're not. What happened?" he asked.

"I've been hit twice. He left me for dead. Help me, Deuce. Let's go home. We'll call a doctor."

"No. No we have to go to the hospital!" exclaimed Deuce.

"No can do, sir. They'll come back and kill me. I know it," he said breathing hard.

"Anything you say boss." Deuce didn't like this but followed Jack Johnson's instructions, explicitly.

"You'll have to sneak the doctor in, telling anyone else I'm dead. I just might be dead anyway," said Jack.

He picked up his boss and took him to the car. He lay him on the back seat and drove away.

The last thing Jack Johnson thought about was his family, specifically, that is if he didn't die he'd pretend that he had. He'd never thought about death before; he didn't like pretend games. He'd been warned and disregarded the warnings. He hadn't played like told so they killed the problem.

Ruth was beside herself for weeks on end. She insisted on a private funeral and no showing of her husband. She'd become hysterical and Fitz thought at any moment he was going to explode and tell his mother everything. She would never forgive him, except he was doing it to save all of their lives. He'd help her later to find a way and then one day she would see him again. Then she would thank him for helping his dad to pull this off. Killers were merciless; he saw it on a regular basis. Even the attorney told him so. His dad had become a hated man, he was too honest and knew too many people in the underworld of this crazy business.

Ruth calmed down and decided that she would move back to New York to be with her daughters and son-in-law and grandbaby. That thought gave her a smile in May as she made plans. Fitz would stay behind and manage the house as it belonged to them and he had a steady job. What he didn't tell her was that Jack had bought him a legal business and he was the full owner. He had hope she might see her husband in the next year or so.

Lucky for Ruth her husband had also been a banker. This saved her in June of 1929. She never saw his body after that fateful day in February. She was lost in oblivion during the short funeral.

She was told he'd died. Later his lawyer gave her his money assets, the amount from the sale of his company and other investments. Ruth rolled her eyes for never did she know how much her husband was worth. She had the money but no Jack.

"Really?"

"Yes, Ruth. And that is after my take from fees with all debts settled. By the way, he had no debts. He paid cash for everything and rarely borrowed. He did inherit the business but managed to grow it exponentially. Here are the titles for property you own in New York City. John and Rose, their young child you've never met I'm told, along with Lilly, live in one of the brownstones near the park. The deed for the home in North Carolina is also enclosed. They are all paid for as well as the property in Florida. I've been told that's the next adventure," said the lawyer.

"Florida?"

"Ruth dear, you seem astonished, like you knew of nothing. It's not my business but you never discussed business, ever?"

"Business? No, never. The weather maybe, but his day, no."

"I see."

"He was extremely private. He studied nightly and we never discussed matters. Once he spoke, that was it. Generous and kind, yes, very private, though," said Ruth. Her mind was racing, racing through their lifetime together. She wished she'd known more but she was busy with children.

"I did know of his generosity and in his will he left several playgrounds, to be built for the school children all around Chicago," he said.

Ruth looked at him. She shivered. Jack never mentioned playgrounds. She wondered what else he'd done.

Tears left her eyes and forcefully sped their way down both cheeks. The lawyer stood and went to her with a kerchief. This was the least he could do. He wished he could bring back her husband.

"Thank you."

"You're welcome. And if you need anything at all I'm here. Here's a business letter with my address and logo," he said.

"What am I to do with all the money?" she asked.

"Well, Ruth, you do have children with bright futures and your help probably wants to stay with you, if and when you move," he said.

"Yes." She paused as in thought. "Emma. Emma has just studied the Tropics in school. The Tropics are in Florida, right?"

"I believe it is a jungle down there of sorts. Certainly, the temperatures are warm, I'm told.

You have three months to sell your holdings in his other companies or you can retain them. They will need your advice, expertise and opinions. Jack was a hands on type of business man."

"I'll check with Fitz. He plans on staying here in Chicago. Emmaline and I are going to New York the first of June, which is next week."

"Sounds good. You know Ruth, he didn't want to sell the spirit business even if it wasn't fully operational but he didn't want you possessing an illegal company if it never was repealed, Prohibition that is."

"Apparently, there is quite a lot I didn't know about my husband. The dear sweet man is the one I'll remember. I'll be in touch when I reach New York for further details, especially about the other businesses. I just may be up to a few challenges which require my judgement and decision making abilities. You know we women are not as brainless as we look," she said, then retracted. "I'm sorry. I'm just in shock."

The large Victorian home on the water remained inhabited by Fitz. A couple of trunks bundled with sentimental items from her late husband and childhood mementos from her children were sent to the summer home in Carolina. She knew she would go there again someday. She just knew she wanted to return to the place where all was quiet and the children ran free and her cares were limited. Maybe they would join her too. One could dream of those days gone by.

Ruth and Emmaline, now 19, took the train back to New York City. Elizabeth, the English nanny had married and moved out soon after Lilly and Rose bounded for New York nearly seven years earlier. DJ and Garrett, the butler and chef, drove two vehicles and would meet them there. While Francis and Deuce, the gardener and horseman turned automobile expert, drove to the summer home. They would keep the place going down there waiting for the family's next trip or vacation. Ruth assured them she would come most likely next summer. It had been too long since she had seen her girls and now she was a grandmother. She felt like time had slipped away and she had some catching up to do. First up was to see Lilly perform and then plenty of hugs and storytelling with reading to her littlest one. That thought brought her pleasure and pain as her husband would never know how his offspring turned out and definitely wouldn't know his grandchildren.

Ruth will never understand her own logic in what she did next. The train stopped at North Depot in Sandusky. For some unknown reason the engineer had his staff go through the cars and explain to the passengers there would be a two hour delay. He apologized but mechanical issues had arisen that needed to be looked at. They assured the passengers it was minor.

Emmaline and her mother Ruth stepped off the train. Passengers were allowed to depart and re board in one hour. They walked through the station with tall ceilings and benches for sitting. Ruth headed for the front doors and walked outside. Emmaline followed. Ruth looked at Emmaline and then over to the Murschel House and the memory flooded her brain. She would tell her dear Emma everything. She had no doubts, no reservations.

"Emma dear, how old are you now?" she asked her daughter.

"Mother, you know, you were there?" replied Emma.

She looked at her daughter and paused, before the past was revealed and forevermore altered Emmaline's view of the postured woman in front of her.

"Your nineteen Emmaline June Johnson and I wasn't there."

The ladies had been walking towards a bench just outside the depot. Emmaline turned to face her mother quickly and sputtered rather crudely, "What's that supposed to mean?"

Ruth Johnson in all her motherly ways could not have predicted a more cold response from her loveliest of daughters. "Please sit."

They sat upon a bench and faced the Murschel house. Ruth began with the letter which had arrived for her nearly seven years ago.

"My dear Emmaline, let me tell you a story, your story. I received a letter on our trip seven years ago when we stopped here headed for Chicago. The orphanage where I found you nineteen years ago had burned down," Ruth began.

Emmaline began to take in the words, *orphanage where I found you*. She was numb. She didn't know how to feel. What was she supposed to feel? Sad? Happy?

"What?"

"Your father did not want you to know that we adopted you from the orphanage. He wanted you to feel a part of the family. Denial I guess."

Emmaline was speechless and wide-eyed. Why was she telling her now?

"And you want to tell me this now because this depot reminds you of a letter? What else is there Mother?" Ruth's eyes misted over.

Ruth used her hand to cover her mouth and lips and slide it over her throat. She needed a moment to hold back the tears she felt were inevitable.

Ruth gasped at a breath of fresh air. "I'm telling you this because you should know. I always wanted to tell you but he didn't. And now he's gone. Truth is always best."

"You weren't there but you are my mother. I love you mom," said Emmaline.

"I love you too. Thanks for that. There's more," Ruth acknowledged.

It was Emmaline who now took the breath and held back tears. Were they tears of fear or betrayal or the unknown? She didn't quite know. Her body shivered. She'd liked or rather loved her dad. But he wasn't her dad? No, he was. It's just that she belonged to someone else and why did they leave her?

"When we came to the orphanage to pick you up you were just a brand new baby. I had just lost a baby in stillbirth. I was devastated. Your father thought it best to adopt and get over it quickly. Your mother, the lady who gave birth to you left two of you but we only took you," Ruth choked. Her tears came rolling down both cheeks. She reached in her pocket for a handkerchief.

"I have a sister or brother. Why did you leave another baby? I'm a twin?" Emmaline began to absorb the enormity of this conversation.

"No honey, but you had an older sister and her

name was Lillian Jean. Your father wouldn't take both so she was left behind." There she said it. The deed was done. Wait. Let it sink in.

Emmaline mouthed the name Lillian Jean just under her breath. Somehow this caused her to smile. She felt funny, almost happy like.

"Mother this is good news. We are headed for New York and I can find my older sister. Now I have three sisters instead of only two!" she exclaimed.

"Yes, except Emmaline, I told you the orphanage burnt down. That's why I received a letter and your father told me to forget about it forever."

"You named the next child Lilly after my sister," replied Emmaline. Emmaline let out a gasp and tears escaped. She didn't know if she was sad or happy. But she trusted her mother.

"Yes, I did. I never wanted to forget about her. I'm so glad I told you. I'm sorry it's too late. Her life was cut short and I suppose it could have been you, too."

"No, no mother, that's not it. Don't you see everything happens for a reason at least that is what the reverend teaches? Your loss and gain was my gain too. Love and heartache brought more love, and now heartache again shall bring us love again."

"Emmaline, you are not making sense. Please explain."

"One of the little old church ladies told me Jesus blesses us with life when there is death. In other words, when someone dies someone else is born. It's like a soul for a soul. The souls cross paths and we are blessed. I'm thinking we are meant to find her now that dad is dead. Of course, I never wanted him to die but now a life is waiting for us. My sister's life is important. Do you think she knows about me?"

"How is it possible Emmaline can turn a terrible story into a happy one?" she asked her daughter. She knew the answer. This was Emmaline, strong, happy and full of adventure. If anyone could find her or have hope that she was still alive it would be her Emmaline.

"I do wish you would have told me sooner. We'll have work to do when we get to New York City." She stated matter-of-factly.

"I guess we will. You are the only one who knows this," said Ruth. She felt relieved for the first time since Lilly was left in the orphanage. Before her own Lilly was born that is all she thought about day and night. She had been too occupied with her own loss but once the brand new baby came there was little time to reflect. Then when she found herself with child after the adoption she gave her littlest one the very name of the one left behind, Lilly. She thought this would make everything better but what it did was give her thoughts and visions which haunted her daily. Around once a week she awoke with a nightmare usually a baby crying or a toddler running through the house screaming.

"I'll find her mother. She needs to know she is wanted and loved."

Chapter 9

John picked up Ruth and Emmaline at the train station on June 2nd, 1929. The city was still bustling with activity, even the stock market was lively with active trading and digits numerically rising. No one knew what lay ahead in the fall, specifically October 24th, which was later called Black Thursday, on Wall Street.

John saw them first and couldn't believe the change in Emmaline. She was a beautiful brunette, no longer wearing pigtails, and quite stunning in stature. He thought to himself she would cause quite a stir wherever she went. His own wife Rose was a beauty for which he never saw another female who could compare. Emmaline just caused him to notice. They would all have such fun getting acquainted again.

"Welcome to New York City!" John exclaimed. He stood behind Ruth Johnson and she turned to see him.

"Thank you John. I'm happy to be back. I wish Jack though was here too."

"I am so sorry for your loss, truly I am. He was a fine man, one of the best."

"Thank you." Ruth closed her eyes for a moment. She didn't want tears, not here, not now.

John turned his attention to her beautiful daughter who stood next to her mother. She wore a dark brown swirl dress which matched the color of her hair. A hat with small plumes accentuated her large brown eyes. She held out her hand, "Hello. I'm Emma. I don't think you remember me. But I remember you very well."

One couldn't help but immediately notice the maturity from her spoken words. She was not only beautiful but confident and contained a strong body when she shook his hand. "One could never forget a girl who supported her little sister in stepping on the big stage at a Christmas party. I do remember you right before your sister Rose whisked me away to show me the snow laden street from her upstairs window."

"Yet it was you who heard the young talent and formulated a plan that we could never have realized in such a little girl of ten years old," Emma replied.

"You think it was all me but your sister Rose is the true blessing in all this. Just wait until you meet your little nieces and nephew," said John.

"I could listen all day but let's go before the heat warms the day. DJ and Garrett are meeting us at the brownstone. Are you positive you have room?" asked Ruth.

"It has four levels, and yes, there is more than enough rooms for all of us. Rose insists you stay at least a year as we have so much catching up to do. She says she could use the help from all of us. We have three children ages two, four, six and one on the way," said John.

"Oh, I didn't know she was with child again," said Ruth. Emma looked delighted.

"That was a slip of my tongue. Please pretend I didn't tell you as that is her big news."

"We will most certainly be surprised at her big news," replied Emma.

"Great then. Let's go. Let me carry your bags. The trunks can go in another vehicle."

DJ and Garrett arrived back at the brownstone before them and assisted with their belongings. The two newcomers would have a whole level for themselves. Rose gave them the upper level with three bedrooms, a bath, and sitting room. She'd made a table area for eating and two small sofas for lounging. The third bedroom would store their belongings for at least a year while mother could look for an appropriate place of residence. Emma settled right in unpacking and preparing her room to her taste, rearranging a few items. She added the bed linens, and pillow cases for the pillows from her room in Chicago. This made her feel at home immediately. She wasn't quite sure what she would do here back in the city of New York when she left Chicago but it didn't worry her a bit. That was Emmaline, ready for the next phase of life. She had studied maps, foreign countries and the tropics, notably Florida, for two years at a university plus piano and tennis.

First though after a few days of catching up with meeting the new family, and of course, seeing Lilly on stage, she would go and join a tennis club. Her mother said she could; said she'd pay for it. After all she was talented in the sport. She would do that first, then see about some sort of employment. What she really wanted to do was go to Florida but not necessarily by herself. It could wait for a bit. *Let me see New York and maybe visit some old friends* she thought.

Rose announced the dinner plans and proceeded to place the toddler and four year old right into Emma's lap. *Emma gave her a look of what shall I do with these?* But that only lasted for a mere glimpse into her present reality. She settled in and began asking questions. "What is your name? And your name, too? Where's your rooms? Do you sleep together? Can I see your toys? Tell me your favorite story!"

Ruth enjoyed getting to know her grandchildren. She had made a couple trips back to see them but had never stayed very long. Had it really been that long since Rose and John left with Lilly? Just then Lilly burst through the front door, full of life like she always had been. Ruth stood as Lilly rushed into her mother's arms.

"Mommy, I've missed you so much. I'm so glad you are here. And Daddy, I miss him too. Why did all that happen to him?" She pleaded for words from her mother for which Ruth could say none. John came over and put his arm around Lilly.

"Sweetie, your mother doesn't know either. She doesn't know if it was tied in with the massacre. She doesn't think so. It seemed to be random, a robbery of some sort. The person got away with cash and left him for dead," John said. He'd told her this before but she couldn't accept it.

"Lilly, someday someone will figure it out or come forth with news. We must stay strong until then. I promise you he loved you and cared about you and your future. He felt blessed by being your dad." Ruth gave her daughter she had let go to pursue a dream seven years ago and only seen a few times since, the longest hug a mother could give. "And, I love you to the moon and back."

Lilly hugged back and exclaimed, "I can't wait until you see me on Broadway. My show is a killer, quite a huge production. My agents, Rose and June, are lining up an audition for a movie. Can you believe it? It's going to have sound, silent movies are going to be history they say." She twirled around with smiles for everyone.

"What's a killer? What kind of show is that?"

"Oh momma, it means it's a knockout!"

Garrett came out with some biscuits and tea and made an announcement to the family gathering. John has decided to take us out for a night on the town, to one of the finest restaurants in the city. Dinner reservations are at eight, but we leave at six thirty for a short tour as it has been many years since you lived here.

The night began a new beginning for the family that had settled beyond the city of New York. They were back minus their leader but ready to begin again. John took them past the Beacon Theatre due to open in December of 1929. Construction was almost finished. He surmised that one day very soon they might be watching their very own Lilly performing in talking movies or live vaudeville performances right here at the Beacon. There was much to discuss that night with the family reunion in the city of their origin.

The very next day DJ took Emmaline to the Tennis Club. Ruth had called on her butler to do this. In lieu of the conversation at the train depot Ruth felt Emmaline, though strong, needed some rest and relaxation. Tennis would surely take her mind off the situation and exercise was good for her body. Emmaline totally agreed and dressed the part. She insisted she stay the whole day and eat her supper there. DJ suddenly had the day off.

Emmaline played several sets of tennis with a fellow member before taking a short break. A lady in the locker room asked if she'd like to play doubles as her partner couldn't make it. "I would love to. What time do you start?"

"Well, if you don't mind we are playing late. That was the only time slot left. We should be finished around eight thirty. Then we are staying for a late dinner. You can join us for that if you'd like," said the lady in the locker room.

"Thanks. That sounds super, love to," replied Emmaline. "I'm Emma by the way, from Chicago."

"I'm Virginia from the state of Virginia," she laughed as it sounded rather funny, "and I recently became a New Yorker. And I love it!"

"Pleased to meet you, wonderful. I'm glad to be

back here as I was born here," replied Emmaline.

"Help me win and I'll buy you drinks. I didn't say that," said Virginia who then winked at her.

"It's a deal Virginia," said Emmaline. She couldn't wait to play twice in the same day.

Later that night after dinner and drinks, after winning in two sets 6-0, 6-0, Emmaline gathered her belongings in the dressing room and checked herself in the mirror. She applied red color to her lips and cheeks, not that she needed any as the day's activities had livened up her circulation and put to rest any paleness. DJ waited in the bar area listening to the music. She opened the back door which led to a hallway before one climbed the stairs to the main level. As she walked she saw a couple kissing and quite engaged at that. There definitely was not enough room to go past them without disturbing their frolic. Certainly they would see her. But they didn't. So she made a clearing of the throat noise, still nothing.

She was in no hurry. She leaned back against the wall then ever so discreetly peeked at the sweet romantic indulgence. She smiled. *To be in love* she thought. She closed her eyes and thought about that thought.

When she heard, "Oh Robert," she looked and for some reason panicked. She yelled, "Fire."

The couple disengaged and looked very disturbed. The woman began running, yelling, "Where? Oh no! Where?"

The man presumably named Robert began to run and follow in her direction but not before he looked back at Emmaline who stared at him. He looked as though he recognized someone. She laughed.

Once upstairs she decided to listen to the music and found herself a seat at the table where DJ was seated. They shared a conversation and she decided she wanted a nightcap before heading home. He ordered one for her, a whiskey in honor of her dad. She sipped it slowly while a man in the shadows watched her intently.

Chapter 10

He figured he would go to the club every day for the next week or two, not to stalk her but to run into her. He didn't want to seem overzealous or act as a madman. Robert wanted to see the girl who was now a woman. She was lovely. Sure, he could look her up or try to find her through his dad. Possibly she moved back here from Chicago. He wanted to find out for himself. For some reason he wanted it to happen naturally and not through his dad who knew everything. His dad had connections like no other human being on earth. *He must not know that they were back here* he thought. Knowing everything came with the territory of the news business. Papers. He sold a lot of them. Robert thought about that for a mere minute. He should go to work for him. How could he possibly deny his father or run off to Florida to meet inventors or other botanists. He loved how the natural world was so beautiful. That was his study, not paper mills and print. Yes, he had to admit who ever invented the printing press and used a real live substance was a miraculous soul! He remembered reading something about wine presses and this may have fostered the idea for a German inventor named Gutenberg.

Why could he not get Emmaline out of his brain? He was twenty one, graduated from Harvard with a Bachelor of Science degree and looking for his first job in the field. He'd written a couple letters to a few scientist and inventors hoping to hear that they needed an associate. That's what he really wanted to do was experiment and research on his own down south away from the wintry weather of the north. He guessed what he really wanted was to branch out on his own away from his very well-known father. How should he tell him? He didn't know. He was the only child and there were expectations, etc. He thought about Emmaline, she probably was doing exactly as she wanted without a care.

Why was she here in New York? He wasn't going to be secretive; he just wanted a fresh chance at an old fashioned, "Hello. How are you?"

Mary Stephens was watching her son as he looked out the kitchen window deep in thought. "More tennis today?"

"Yes Mother. I want to play as much as I can. It

freshens my thought and I know once I get to work it won't happen as often."

"You should have a wonderful time this summer, take the whole three months off and make your decision in August. See what you find out there. You can always work for your father. You know that, right?"

"Sure, but I don't want to let him down."

"He would love to have you and maybe that is what you will decide in the end. It's your decision. Possibly I'll take your place and go to work for him. That will let you off the hook!"

They both laughed. She meant every word though. She knew her son wanted to go far away. She hoped he would come back someday.

"See you later tonight after dinner," he said going out the door.

"I'll save dinner for you," she said.

"Don't bother I'm eating at the club."

"I'll put your mail on your desk in the study. It will be there when you come home tonight," she said.

"Great. I have my mail to look forward to tonight. Perfect. Have a good day, mother," Robert said and left.

Lilly, Rose and Emmaline went shopping for new dresses in a fashionable section of New York.

They couldn't finish in one day, so they went the next day and the day after that. Finally, Emmaline said to her sisters, "Tomorrow ladies I must return to the tennis club. I believe I saw someone I used to know. It's intrigued me to no end."

"Sister, do tell. Who is it?" Lilly asked exuberantly.

"I'm not sure. I'll tell you when I know," she responded.

"Is he handsome or rich or both?" asked Rose.

"What on earth are you saying?" Emmaline asked.

"Well, give me a description of someone you admire. I'd like to know. Tell. Tell."

"Rose dear, you have the most handsome husband around, no one compares to the dashing John."

"But what do you like?" she persisted.

She thought for a moment and stopped in front of a store. She noticed her reflection in the mirror.

"I do believe it is more than looks or money that which attracts me to a person. This man has an edge, a quality almost indescribable. It is as though we are two pieces, two trees in the wind blowing in the same direction, receiving the same storm. When the sun comes out we both shine, and likely in the midst of winter when skies are gray blue and the utter stillness of night descends upon the forest, we become company for each other. We are not alone but strength for each other side by side."

The sisters looked at their Emmaline. They were stilled. Stunned. Silence broken by arms that wrapped around her, held tight by a group hug only seen by the glass reflected back out to the street. In this moment, Emmaline knew she was different, she thought different and acted different. What on earth did she really want?

She would travel miles and miles before she found that answer. When you look for something that is unknown you really aren't looking for anything she determined, just an adventure. She needed adventure, the unknown, to feel she was alive and living.

"Emmaline, you best get to that club tonight and play some tennis to clear your thoughts and of course, find Mr. Tree," said Lilly. They laughed, and laughed some more holding arms as they walked down the avenue.

Before Emmaline left for the club Ruth called her in to her private salon. She slept there and they both sat on a small loveseat made of burgundy velvet. "What is it mother?"

"I have found out a bit of news and am not sure if it will be helpful," said Ruth.

"Go on, I'm listening. I've decided not to tell

anyone about this subject until I've found out all I can. I appreciate your silence mother," said Emmaline.

"Yes. I think that best also. Then when you know everything you can talk with your sisters and brother."

Emmaline held her mother's hands.

"This is not the best information but it does come from a very reliable source. I was told that a certain person who can be trusted over heard a conversation down in Florida at a fancy hotel in Saint Augustine."

"Yes, and what was said?"

"A man bragged to another man that he brought his wife to Florida after he bought her at an orphanage right before it burned down a week later," Ruth said. She managed to get the whole repulsive truth out in one sentence.

"That's Florida, not New York," she stated.

"Emmaline, the man was from New York and he also said he did this more than five years ago."

"Where is he now?" she asked.

"I don't know, but I can give you the hotel name. You cannot travel there yourself, it's far too dangerous!" exclaimed Ruth. But how did she know. She really didn't.

Later on after playing a set of tennis, as it was

too late and getting dark, she freshened up and made her way to the lounge area for a light dinner and maybe a drink. Certain waiters offered special drinks especially since it was a private club.

That's when she saw him sitting alone at the bar. She gathered her wits and didn't even think about what she was doing. His back was to her.

"Did you find the fire?" she inquired.

He looked and there she was right in front of him. "I didn't, but I did find you."

She'd figured it out, too, just like he had.

Chapter 11

He gave her a look of immense approval before he glanced her over from head to toe. "My, my, darling Emmaline. I've thought about you from time to time, actually, quite a bit."

It was her turn. She took a deep breath, smiled and felt flattered. "Robert, my adventurer, you are a sight and maybe relief to these traveling eyes who don't know where to look next."

He didn't know quite how to take that, so he took it as a compliment and moved forward. "May I buy you dinner? There's a back room where we can dine just for patrons."

"Absolutely, I'm starved. Thirsty too!"

He didn't know why he did this but he took her hand and walked her through the main room, then down a hallway and found the back room. There were a couple tables filled but otherwise empty. He found a nice quiet table near a window which looked out over a small lake. It was partially lit by the moon.

"No fire back here but we practically have the place to ourselves." Indeed they did.

"Tell me everything that has happened since 1922." She demanded.

"Emmaline that is seven years. You want it all since we swam in the secret pool."

"Yes. Robert, oh I miss that pool. I almost forgot."

"We should go back there someday," he stated.

"Yes, we should." She instantly thought about finding her lost sister. Should she tell him? She wondered. She looked lost in thought.

"Emmaline, I mean to go to Florida. I'm looking at that right now, maybe before the summer is out," he said.

"Florida? What for?" She asked.

"I didn't think you were listening."

"Sorry, I received some news today and I'm figuring out what to do about it." She stared at him. This really wasn't the time to be discussing family business as she had just met him after all these years.

"I can tell it must be serious. You don't have to tell me now. Let's catch up, then after dinner if you want to talk, I'm here."

She remembered he was always so logical, methodical. Understanding. Emmaline smiled and ordered her Father's best bourbon that she knew he drank. Robert ordered the same. The evening was off to a great start.

The table remained noisy with conversation, never a lack of words shared between the pair that had just reunited after seven years. They shared laughter and accomplishments and finally the death of her father and the loss of his business.

"That's why we came back to New York, but Fitz stayed in Chicago with the house. Mother is going to run a couple of his side businesses as best she can. She'll have John to help her. Which leaves me and what am I going to do? Certainly I cannot play tennis every day of my life," she laughed.

"Sounds like we're in the same boat."

She looked at him and nodded her head in agreement.

"Would you like to go and listen to some live music tonight?" He asked.

"Why not?"

"First though, I need to stop at my place which is my folks place, and retrieve my mail. It's important. I'm expecting some news today," he stated.

They left the club and stopped by his place, then went on their way to the local jazz scene around the corner. The joint was lively, smoky and definitely melodic with a bluesy singer on stage. Once seated he pulled out his letter and said, "Do you mind?"

"Go ahead, read your news you've been waiting on."

It was exactly what he had been waiting for and more. He was elated. He was happy. But in a cross hair of a moment he quieted himself, he didn't want to lose out on the very beautiful young woman named Emmaline Johnson.

"Well, what does it say? Who is it from? Where will you be working?" Her inquisition was forthright and ended with a smile.

He paused. He ordered a drink. He looked at her.

"Okay Robert Stephens from New York City by way of Harvard these past four years, let me read it," she demanded.

What the hell. He handed it to her...

"I'm going with you!"

He looked surprised. "What?"

"I mean let me go with you. I need to go to Florida to look for my sister," she blurted out.

"Your sister? Which one?"

"The one I've never met," she said. She should cry or something. But the soft rain let out via the cheek didn't come. There was too much work to be done. Instead she gathered her emotions and smiled.

"Please tell me," he said.

"Robert, apparently I have a sister who was in the orphanage with me as an infant. I was adopted and she was left behind. I know it sounds cruel but they had their reasons. Except he'll never be able to tell me what they were. Mother kept the secret because she had to. I just found out when we were coming back to New York."

"A sister, really? Where do you think she is?"

"St. Augustine."

"I'll be passing through there eventually on my way down to the end of Florida or as far as I can go. Are you sure you are up for the territory? It may be rough, very rough."

"You'll be there, you're the botanist. You will protect us from the dangers lurking in the marshes or swamps. Right?"

"Do we need permission from your mother to go? I mean we'll be together and not married."

"Mother will give me permission and I'll borrow a ring to place on my finger in case of suspicious or nosy characters. It will be an adventure! And I'll get to look for my sister and you will get to meet and study with the best inventors in the world!" Emmaline was truly delighted. She couldn't think of anything else.

Robert pulled out an envelope from his pocket. It was very small. "This though takes us to a special place. We'll get to visit our summer homes for a brief visit on the way."

"What is it?" She couldn't fathom any more surprises.

"An invitation to a party in Asheville. My father knows someone who will be there and he has asked to meet me. It is supposed to be a grand place. We'll both go. I need a date to be with me as everyone will have wives there, I'm sure."

"A trip on a train, a visit to our old summer homes, a grand party invite, an adventure to Florida and the possibility of meeting my sister seems like a dream come true. When do we leave?"

"Sooner versus later, my darling Emmaline. But you must first ask your lovely mother. She will miss you and this trip could take three to six months."

Chapter 12

Emmaline could not sleep. She tossed and turned then laid awake looking out the window. She would miss her mother but she felt like her whole world had suddenly opened up and she was not going to hesitate. Being with Robert felt nice and comfortable. They were friends. Neither had even a glint in their eyes or did they? If they did, neither recognized it as yet.

Petals must have suspected her awake as he came into the room and lay next to her bed. The next thing she knew her cat named London jumped upon the bed like the prowler she was and meowed quietly while advancing towards Emma's head. She reached her hand down to pet her, then her pretty cat purred soft and sweet like romantic music.

"Yes, I'll miss both of you but I will be back. Take care of momma for me."

"I can take care of myself," whispered Ruth back

at her. "Besides, I have Rose and she is the mother of us all."

"That's the truth momma. And her husband takes care of her like it's his business," said Emmaline.

They both giggled just a little. Then she turned serious. "Momma, I will be back but probably only to visit. You need to know that. I will be going away for good, eventually."

"Emmaline, you must be proper when traveling. Always be a lady first then quietly do your business, whatever that is," ushered Ruth.

"We will momma. You can come visit or live with us if we stay down in Florida."

"First have your adventure, then summon me," Ruth meant every word. "For now, Lilly needs me as she is about to begin her adult career on the stage. Her reviews have been stellar. It's going to happen very soon. Then she may be traveling far and wide. I'll have to go with her I suspect."

"I can't wait to read about her in the paper momma. You won't ever read about me in the paper. My work will be behind the scenes, exploring, building or discovering, I think. Faraway places with peace and simplicity."

Ruth looked over at her daughter and sighed. Where she got that spirit and knowhow, Ruth knew it wasn't from her. She would have liked to have met her daughter's mother, even the father. Ruth decided right then and there in the middle of the night she would investigate. Then maybe someday she could tell Emmaline why she was the way she was. Ruth fell asleep knowing that she would accomplish this with the help of Rose's husband, the lawyer. He knew everything.

In the morning before they left the brownstone to meet Robert at the station, Ruth stopped Emmaline and demanded her attention.

"What, mother?"

Ruth took her wedding ring and placed it on Emmaline's finger. "I want you to wear this. This is what you need to travel so many miles together."

"You are right. It's a perfect fit. Now I feel like I'm undercover or something. I have to pretend to be married. What an adventure! Guess I'm an actress now," said Emmaline. She put lipstick on and pursed her lips. Come to think of it she felt light like a butterfly. Her stomach even quivered slightly.

It had been decided that Garrett would be accompanying the duo on this trip. Everyone felt relieved with his more than enthusiastic response of, "Yes, mam I'd love to go on the adventure with Emmaline and Robert. That is to say Mr. and Mrs. Robert Stephens."

Rose and Ruth would be cooking while he

attended the pair to Florida and back. Emma and Robert were old enough to travel alone, but going so far to unknown territory made both families feel better.

When Emmaline arrived at the station with her three pieces of luggage, Robert was there to assist her. They found a place to rest before the departure. Respectfully they said good bye to their families. Mary and Charles Stephens shook hands and exchanged hugs with Ruth Johnson. It had been awhile and they needed to catch up with each other. The threesome left the station and went to breakfast at a local diner. Ruth knew she could ask Charles about where to start in her search for Emma and Lilly's mother. First she had to tell him the story and also fill him in on the death of her husband. He knew about it just not the details.

Robert and Emmaline were traveling first class, at least it seemed that way to them. They had a room with beds and a freshening station along with two small sofas below. A large window looked out at the scenery. Emma smiled and began testing everything out, sitting here and there and even attempting to climb up to the bed. Garrett held a room not far from theirs.

"Wait, check it out later. Let's go find our dinner table," said Robert.

She laughed. "You're right, let's go.'

"Remember, we are married," he laughed.

"Do we have to kiss in public?" she mused.

He just looked at her. He didn't know what to say.

Chapter 13

The Atlantic Coast Line Railroad was well serviced with plenty of staff to meet the needs of its travelers. They'd be boarding that train line after Asheville. For now they made their way to Richmond, Virginia.

After lunch the pair settled back to the stateroom and began a lengthy discussion. Robert was twenty one and Emmaline just nineteen, both were adventurous and schooled but a bit naive. Eager to set out in the world and both still under their families expenses. That was okay for now. They began talking about how they would make their way in the world.

"I want to make something, something from nature, possibly out of the tree that produces the flex substance called rubber," Robert began.

"I want to build something, something that lasts, in a new place where no one has been before. Maybe we can discover a new place, you and me," she said.

"My dad says there has never been a better time to invent something. Inventions and patents are conceived every day. He has put me in touch with a couple colleagues of his from the paper," Robert reported.

"Is that who you are going to meet in Asheville?" she asked.

"Yes, it will be informal because the affair is a large party celebrating some professor who is retiring from a college down south. But we will get to mingle with the guests and meet my father's friends."

"I'm very excited to see the place. I've heard about its grandeur and once I saw a picture of the place. Unbelievable that one family resides there. Fascinating," Emmaline said. She turned and looked out the window thinking about some of the places she studied in school. Most of the castles, large churches and magnificent homes were in Europe. She didn't think she'd ever get over there to see them, so this was going to be a real treat!

The young couple pretending to be married on the train received luxurious amenities, between the food and service. A young waiter served them their dinner and they befriended him telling him of their adventure to the south, but not of their marriage pretension.

"Don't tell anyone I mentioned this but please enjoy all this service on the train line. I just heard that in two weeks on July 1st the whole line is striking. I may not have a job for a while," said the young man.

The couple looked at one another. "Seriously, you know this. It may be fact, not hearsay?"

"Let's say I heard it from the top. That is all," said the young man. "The train will still run for the most part, they think, just without service."

"Thank you for letting us know. You didn't have to tell us all that," said Emmaline.

"I just didn't want you all to get stranded on your adventure," said the waiter.

"Yes, thanks. We do want to get back home someday, right sugar?" he said and smirked.

"O dear, yes. Our families want us back home in New York."

Later that night Robert pulled out a flask and poured him and Emmaline a small swirl of bourbon his dad had given him. She coughed slightly but drank it anyway. This would be her first night sleeping on the train in the same room as him.

"Emma, my dad says Pearl will give us information as to where the man moved to. She managed to talk with him after she heard it was New York where he was from. What on earth moved her to pay attention I don't know? But I'm sure it's going to lead us to your sister Lilly."

"I'm not worried at all Robert. My mother even gave me money to buy chocolate for Lilly. That's how much she believes we are going to find her. She found out that her mother worked in a chocolate factory; though, that is about all mother remembers or knows."

Robert looked at Emmaline and smiled warmly. She returned the outward embrace in like. "You'll need to leave now while I get ready for bed and settle in this top bunk."

Robert sat at the table and reviewed the trip on his map. They would change trains in Richmond, then on to North Carolina where they'd get off the train and his father's hired hands would pick them up to go to the summer home for a week. From there they would load their belongings and go to Asheville for the party. They had been invited to stay one or two nights in the large European inspired chateau. That was a surprise he was keeping from Emmaline. He was sure she'd love that. He smiled. He was excited too just like her. He had never planned on this trip, especially with such a beautiful young lady that he had adored when both were just children. He wasn't even sure how long they would be gone but possibly they'd be home by fall, October or so, maybe even September. What if the train stopped working? He shook his head and went back to the room. Emmaline was already asleep.

They had a stop in Richmond and changed train lines. It would be two hours before their train would depart. Emmaline spied a couple shops across the street and wanted to look around. Robert decided to go with her. The street was crazy. There were automobiles driving every which way and hitching posts for horses around the corner.

One had a sense that time stood still here in this city that bordered the south and its agriculture. Emmaline walked quickly with Robert crossing the street before another auto careened from around the corner. The two of them stepped inside Ginny's Rail House to look around. It wasn't just a grocery store or a clothing store but had an assortment of wares. Emmaline walked over to the candy selection and bought a small box of chocolates made in Ohio. The store owner said they had just arrived the other day. She said they were homemade Swiss chocolates just like the ones made in Europe. Some guy from Ohio named Harry London had a brand new business and she was almost sold out.

Emmaline paid the money and asked her for extra paper to wrap them in as she had a long journey before she could deliver them. The lady assured her they would be fresh as she'd just bought them a day ago. Robert looked around and bought a knife; he thought he might need it at some point but wasn't sure when that might be. His dad always told him to carry one and so now he did. Maybe he'd have to protect himself and Emmaline. He shrugged that thought immediately when he looked over at her.

Three more days of travel by train and automobile and they arrived to a place they remembered so well. The Johnson's summer home was closed but Charles made sure that the pair would be welcomed to his place for the week. As soon as Robert came up with his plan to travel south his father had opened up the place by employing two local hands to prepare it. The hired hands had been there for two weeks preparing the place, cleaning up the dust, doing the laundry, and purchasing the groceries. Charles asked them to stay for the summer as he and Mary would come later this summer. It had been a few years since they had summered there. Mary mentioned to Robert they'd like to meet them there if it worked out possibly at the end of summer.

There was no pretending now that the couple was out of sight. In fact, they could be themselves and they did just that occupying separate rooms, reading, or even eating when they felt like it. Cordial was more like it until one day Robert reminded Emmaline of the swimming pool.

Chapter 14

"The swimming poooooool," she murmured. "Oh yes, I remember that. We kept it our secret and never told a soul." Emmaline looked up and over at him. She paused and glanced at Robert lingering for a moment at his shoulders and then at his face, specifically his mouth and jaw. She caught herself and looked up at his eyes which were chocolate brown and staring at her. The moment was noted between both individuals. Uncertainty belied their feelings as they readjusted their stance. Emmaline, who had been sitting rose to go near the window where Robert stood. He gazed out the window and reflected those days gone by given away as youthful desire for fun.

He turned and met her gaze again. "We should see what all the fuss worth hiding was all about."

"I like that idea. Probably, it's abandoned and dry."

"After all Miss Emmaline, this is a first class adventure we're on. I'll follow the leader." He winked at her.

"Leader? You've got the pants on, you're the leader!"

"You can borrow mine," he said.

She put her hands on her hips in a gesture of impatience and replied, "I will do just that. I'll borrow the corduroy knickers if you don't mind."

"Those are my riding pants," he said flustered.

"Perfect, we should ride horses to the destination if we can remember how to get there."

"Great idea, I'll have the guy's saddle up a couple of mares after lunch."

"Have them bring a paper too so we can check on the train strike," said Emmaline. "Maybe we should get a head start instead of spending a week here in the mountains," she relayed.

"I like the way you think Miss Emmaline. We can spend more time here on the way back after we reach our southern destinations."

Robert had the hired hands saddle up a couple horses they had brought with them. He asked them to bring a paper next time they went to town for supplies. They replied they were going in today, later this afternoon. Did he need anything else they inquired?

He thanked them for asking and told them yes he needed a few supplies. He thought he would make Emmaline a special dinner. It would be his special gift, something he could do to make this trip a nice affair for both of them. Pearl had taught him how to make a special pork barbeque outside over a fire when the inside stove went out. He'd make her dinner tonight when they got back from the swimming pool. *She'd like that* he thought.

Emmaline climbed up on her horse with ease. She was wearing Robert's trousers and found everything quite easy to do. He did the same. The pair departed for the way to the lake, but keen on what lay before the lake. How long had it been?

"It's only been ten years but it seems so much longer, I'm afraid."

"All I can think about is where I'm going next. I never think about that lifetime except now with you," Robert said thoughtfully.

She smiled. He was kind. He was handsome as she had noted earlier today. Now he said something about being with her. She felt nice all of a sudden.

Emmaline was doing exactly what she wanted. She was riding a horse with pants on going to God knows where to find something out of their past. Sounds adventurous, even to her.

Robert liked her in the lead. They rode head to

tail with her up front. He enjoyed watching her hair fall and hips move in the saddle as the horse walked and paved the path. Every now and then when she looked behind her he would point in the direction he thought they should travel. He did bring a map. He was not going to get lost and frankly did not want to sleep out here in the tall grass or woods. He took his adventurous spirit only so far. Maybe it was his upbringing in the fine city of New York but he traveled well with fine clothes purchased by his parents. In his youth he camped with his dad but that was then. He loved the plants and outdoors but also liked his bed. *He was the only child and his dad did well, not as well as Emmaline's but at least it was legal* he thought. He was not opposed to drinking liquor, everybody did it, as it was everywhere. But his dad ran a tidy news business and Robert did not want to disappoint him with any wrong doings.

The couple made it to the lake first and took a dip in the cool water. It was June and very hot. This gave them time to gather their bearings about the location of the pool.

"I'm sorry about your father Emmaline. Do you miss him?" he asked.

"Yes," she uttered.

"Of course, you do. I'm sorry. Terrible question I know."

"That's okay. I don't mind answering," she responded.

"I do miss him but I have my mother and she's terrific. But somehow, I think I would have ended up working for him someday. I liked how he managed so many businesses. He was so capable."

"I do know what you mean. I'm going out on my own but my dad's paper business is always there. I may end up working for him. So I know how that feels. I suppose that is security, a backup plan."

"Robert, being adventurous like us is good. We want more than securing onto what has always been. With our dads being so stable it gives us an edge; we can conquer a little of the world all on our own. We can go back anytime."

"Knowing we can go back is a comfort. But we are not ready for that."

"Lilly didn't have a dad or a mom. I wonder how she made it. I wonder if she's okay. What if she's not? What if she's already dead?"

Robert looked over at his strong, beautiful companion and could tell she was on the verge of tears. He walked through the water and went over to her. He didn't know what he was going to do.

"She's not. I just know it. Why would a guy take her out of an orphanage and bring her down to Florida? To hurt her? That doesn't make sense."

"You're too kind. She might not be dead but that doesn't mean he hasn't hurt her."

"What if she doesn't want to come back with us? What if she's happy where she is? Can you let her be?" he asked.

"I will let her be, let her go. I just want to meet her, to know her!" she exclaimed.

Why he did this he didn't know. He hadn't planned on it. He reached out and touched her tears and wiped them away. She let him.

Robert told her about the special dinner he was making for both of them tonight. They decided not to stop at the pool today. They'd save it for tomorrow.

Emmaline wanted Robert to lead them back to his summer home so she could just sit atop her horse and not worry about the trail. He led them back and took a different path back which went right past her summer place. She had no desire to go inside. It had been locked up for several years now and probably needed a good dusting off. Her mother would take care of that. She said she might even come down when the Stephens came down later this summer or fall. *It might just work out* she thought *that everyone would be down later this summer or early fall, everyone except her father.*

She looked over to the front of the homestead

with curtains still in the window and porch furniture as they left it. Where was mother's garden? She looked around, she couldn't find it. As they passed the south side of the home she looked again.

"What are you looking for Emma?"

"Mother's garden."

"I believe the snows down here would have killed it all. It's probably overgrown, that is why you cannot find it. We'll look when we return. Maybe then your family will be here too."

Emmaline felt a chill climb up her spine. She shivered. "I'm ready for that fire and whatever you are cooking for me Mr. Stephens."

"I aim to please tonight Mrs. Stephens," he said and they both laughed a loud.

Emmaline and Robert both missed her mother's garden which existed just down the hill on the south side of the homestead and definitely not full of weeds. They would both miss the curtain pulled back on the second floor while apparently someone watched them and their horses make it back to the Stephens barn.

"I've been thinking about what you said and look here at the paper."

"The Atlantic Coast Line Railroad Will Strike," she read the headlines aloud. "What should we do?"

"They could strike for an indefinite amount

of time. Remember what the worker said, they'd probably still run just no host services," he said.

"We could do without service but if it stopped we'd be stuck for who knows how long. I don't mind getting stuck as long as it's where I want to be. How about you?"

"I'm with you Emma. Let's get to where we want to be!"

It was decided that night they would not stay for a week. They would depart the day after tomorrow. Tomorrow they would go to the pool and leave the next day.

Chapter 15

While Emmaline washed up and napped a short while Robert cut his ingredients and prepped for the sauce to go with his pork he'd had the hands purchase. He cured the pork with salt and pepper then rolled it in fine chicken wire. He had the hands help with building him a mighty hot fire outside. He'd put that over and above some coals and let it cook slowly for a few hours. Then he came back and prepared his special sauce, rather Pearl's special delight. He remembered how wonderful her lemonade was too.

Suddenly it hit him right there in the kitchen. She had made his family special like it was her own. He felt the smile reveal across his face. He and Emmaline were going to see her in a week or so.

"Tell me, tell me! What is the smile on your face for?"

"He looked at her and paused, "My Miss

Emmaline, you look wonderful, better than anything I've cooked up for you tonight."

"Sir, the smile? I want to know what pleases you so."

"Oh, I was thinking about Pearl and how she cooked for us all those years. She gave us her heart in a way. That made me smile and the fact that we will see her in a week down in St. Augustine."

"Pearl, I remember Pearl. She made the best lemonade and sometimes she mixed it with sweet tea. Right!?"

"Yes, you do remember." Robert straightened up his stance and breathed a sigh. "She packed us lunches for the lake."

"Ah yes, can I help?"

"If you'd like you can take a couple blankets out by the fire and set up an area where we can eat this fine southern wood style barbeque by way of Pearl the cook."

"Sounds good." He stared after her as she had put on a summer dress with straps barely there and the skirt of her dress shimmered and swayed as she walked. He swore she looked more beautiful than anyone in all the world. But what did he know? Nothing, he swore at himself.

Robert cut the tomatoes, measured some vinegar and molasses, and added brown sugar to the saucepan over the inside stove. Mustard seed and a few other small spices were shaken in and, of course, some cooking wine. It already smelled delicious but this would take about an hour to simmer and meld together. He gathered some dishes and glasses and joined Emmaline near the fire.

"I'll be right back. I must retrieve something from the barn." He vanished for a moment.

She pondered what he was up to and couldn't think of anything.

He reappeared with a bottle. "If you'd like a glass of wine I have it for you. But you don't have to drink anything if you don't want."

"Mr. Stephens, yes I'd love a glass. It looks like red wine."

"Don't ask me how I got a bottle of red Bordeaux from France all the way here to North Carolina. But I did." Robert chuckled.

Wide eyed Emmaline was now more curious than ever. "Please, please tell!"

"A man like a woman must not give up all his secrets, elsewhere we wouldn't look so superior at times," he muttered out.

"Okay, keep your secret. But remember, we work as a team you and I. We go way back," she said slyly.

Robert poured them both a glass and presented a toast to Emmaline. "Here's to way back."

"To way back," she toasted.

The fire was hot but they weren't to close as the night was warm yet. The sun was almost set behind the mountains. Colors were beginning to paint the sky. The cooler air was an hour away. Emmaline smiled for no apparent reason. Robert looked over at her. He smiled at her.

He set his glass down and took hers from her hand setting it on a small outdoor wooden table. Then he leaned over and with his hand lifted her chin towards him. What was he doing? He didn't know. She closed her eyes and he kissed her softly for a good while.

This was a moment Emmaline dreamed about every now and then, not too frequently, but when she was taken with someone. This had happened a couple times now when she had been in school and fell for a boy in another class. She'd never talked with them only dreamed about them and how she'd like to kiss them.

He kissed her again and they fell to the earth below them. This went on for a while until suddenly Robert remembered the sauce.

"Watch the fire, I have something on the stove inside. Be right back."

She laughed and so did he.

They ate dinner fireside and drank half a glass of

wine. He took the rest inside where she joined him. His barbeque turned out well and he surprised her with a desert from in town made by a local baker.

They finished the wine upstairs where Emmaline tried on the real Mrs. Stephens hats from a generation ago. Frilly Victorian pieces from Robert's grandmother entertained them while they finished the wine. Robert turned on a small Victrola which played some swing music. He took Emmeline's arms and began to swing her to and fro, dancing together up in the bedroom belonging to his parents.

Laughing, embracing and enjoying one another the two eventually landed upon the bed and fell asleep.

"I forgot to share this with you last night. I was saving it for a special occasion and last night seemed to fit that bill. Here, look." He handed her an invitation.

"What is this?" She opened the small letter and read the enclosure.

He waited for her to read it, then responded.

"What do you think?"

"Robert, we don't have anything to wear to a chateau. I mean it's a mansion. I've heard it's bigger than a hotel!" She exclaimed.

"Well, I've never seen it but I've heard it's extraordinaire. And we get to go, stay overnight and attend a party. We are going in my father's place. It's all been arranged."

"Are we still married?" She had to ask.

"Not for this party, just engaged," he replied. "We will be in separate rooms."

"We are so proper in proper society," she laughed. "Seriously, we must act accordingly. What do you hope to reach or obtain by attending this soiree?"

"I'm representing my father, the paper business. So its light, more of a social gathering but I'll get to meet some people that might be interested in a future endeavor. Maybe you will be interested in a future endeavor, maybe something in the south. Some people have made money they want to invest it in opportunities and Florida is a 'pardon my expression' a land of opportunity."

"Opportunity. Florida. I've wanted to go to the Tropics for so long now. Robert, I can't believe it. We both are going where I've wanted to go for a long time now!"

He hugged her and she hugged him back.

And just maybe we'll find your sister he thought.

Chapter 16

The pair rode off on their horses to find the pool they swam in over ten years ago. Who did it belong to? And were they still the owners? It didn't matter; they'd know soon enough.

Today they skipped the lake and headed right for the pool. Robert and Emmaline tied up the horses to a tree in the woods.

Being older the couple thought more about the intrusion onto other people's property. "We need to be careful, so no one shoots at us thinking we are robbers or something."

"You are right Robert. I hadn't thought of that. Why are we suddenly feeling rather foolish and not so brave?"

"Because we know more now that we are adults. I'm twenty-one and you are nineteen. We should know better than to sneak unto someone's property and swim in their pool. Right?"

"Right. Maybe we should come at night when for sure no one would be here."

He thought about that and then he thought about his whole future unfolding and depending upon this trip south. "Let's be sneaky. We'll just tell them, if caught, that we came to see our childhood place where we played all summer long."

"How could they deny us a look into our past, right?"

"Still, be prepared to run and fast. Okay darling?" He asked her and begged with his eyes for her to be willing to do this.

"And quiet my dear. We must be quiet so no one hears a sound from us."

Quickly they found the old stairs laden with green moss and weeds. It was still there. They climbed upon the green carpet stealthily like they were in search of gold.

At the last step and before Robert could look over the perimeter, he turned and held out his hand for Emmaline. Today she was his partner in crime.

She reached for his hand and steadied herself. She became light and giggled ever so quietly. He looked back and smiled himself. What on earth were they doing?

The two of them made their way across the greenery towards the pool. They didn't see or hear a soul. Upon reaching the brick path around the pool the discovery was finalized. To their amazement the pool was filled with fresh sparkling water. They looked in and it was clear, clean all the way to the bottom.

They looked at one another and didn't remember it being so clean. Were they thinking the same thing? Somebody was home. Somebody had cleaned the pool.

Robert took Emmaline's hand. "We must look around first before we swim."

She readily agreed. They went further past the shrubbery and planted trees that had grown so big in ten years. They kept walking towards what they hoped might expose a home or something. Robert found a path. Emmaline shrugged her shoulders and sighed. Just a little ways she told herself, then she was retreating.

Robert saw it first what looked like a small cottage or tiny house. "Maybe this is a storage house or shed."

"What if someone is in there? We are trespassing!"

"I never saw a sign. Did you?"

"Robert, I'm scared."

"One little look. Let's listen near the window." And so they took a moment and listened. They heard nothing. Robert looked in the window, then he went to the door and tried the knob.

It opened.

Emmaline's eyes were wide and she was not about to blink. She had to be ready, just in case she had to run and run fast.

"Follow me," he said. He went inside and saw the containers. Liquor.

Emily looked transfixed. She knew what this was. Her own father had been in the business of selling liquor, even during Prohibition. No one had to tell her. It was quite apparent. Even her mother knew. But what was she going to do call the cops on her own husband and turn him in after years of family traditions in selling fine liquors? No, that's why he had to move to Chicago where he wouldn't get caught. The big guys called him there. She knew that. He had to work for them, temporarily. Temporarily, that was a word her father used to use quite often.

"You, okay? You look like you've seen a ghost."

"Yeah, this reminds me of my father and his sales."

"Emmaline, this is small stuff, peanuts if you will."

"Rum-running."

"Rum-running?"

"Someone nearby is bootlegging this out of here.

This here is their extra private stash."

"How do you know?"

"Newspapers," he replied.

"Newspapers?"

"My dad did an article on bootlegging, not to report or get anybody in trouble, but because we all know many people partake in the liquor by being rather quiet about it. He just reported about how people make the stuff. They need water like the pool and a way to get it out of here."

"How do they get it out of here?" She wanted to know. She should read more papers she decided. She needed to know the real deal of what goes on.

"I'm working on that. I'm not sure yet. But I do think if we follow that path it will lead right to the center of the operation."

"The center of the operation? That means people, bootleggers?"

She wanted to escape right now. He wanted to see more. His father's profession was influencing him at this moment.

"One little peek, I promise. Then we'll go, jump in the pool and off we go back to the safety of our summer homes where we are just normal people not looking for adventure."

When they followed the path they didn't find what they might expect. Of course, they weren't sure what they were supposed to find. But maybe a big house with people or something besides the two large open air shacks in front of them. No one was here but all the equipment of running an operation was totally intact. It seemed as though someone had taken the day off or simply went to deliver their goods.

Robert saw the dirt road out a ways and walked towards it. She followed right behind, not wanting to be left alone or him not in site. Yes, she was afraid.

There were no vehicles in any direction but definitely tire tracks of all sorts were seen both ways.

"This seems to be the back of someone's property. Remember when we had those maps and the pool seemed to be at the edge of the neighbors land. The main house must be up around the bend of this dirt road."

"This road is small, very narrow and not well seen with its twists and turns."

"Probably so not to cause concern for an illegal operation, my dear."

"What do we do now?" She asked.

"We swim."

They laughed as they ran back to the pool. Robert hid behind a tree and told her, "Don't look."

"What are you doing?"

"You gave me the idea. You heard about it when

passing through Ohio on the train. Remember?"

"Oh, the naked swimmers at the park!" she remembered.

"Join me."

She raced behind a tree and took everything off. Smiling she said, "Close your eyes, I insist." Then she ran to the pool and jumped in making a splash.

The water felt fine. She should have tested it first but there was no time. For a few minutes they relaxed and swam around in the clean and clear water. He assumed it was mountain water from a nearby stream.

Emmaline swam to the edge and held on. She caught her breath and began to feel exhilarated. She wished this moment might last longer. He did too. Robert swam over near her and reached out to hold onto the ledge also.

Their faces were close, their breaths loud and hair completely wet. "You look beautiful, you know."

She could only look back at him and words eluded her while her thoughts stood frozen. She wanted to kiss him again. And so she did. He held her wet face and drew her even closer forgetting they had nothing on.

The kiss lasted a lifetime. Seriously, neither one wanted it to end. Finally when the sweet taste of Robert was more than she could take or else she might faint, they parted lips. She began to think of the summers they played and secretly went swimming right here. They had no idea it was a bootlegger's hideout.

He held her face in his hands and felt the closeness of her naked body. *This might be the most delirious he'd ever been* he thought. For sure, it was the best date in all the world. He would never forget his skinny dipping date with the girl named Emmaline from his youth.

"Emmaline, I'll get out first. Then you go dry off and get dressed. I'm going to partake in a bottle for our trip to paradise. I mean down south."

He was up and out before she could take notice or be concerned. Her turn. She swam to the steps over by the side, then hurried to the tree to dress.

Once they mounted their horses and began the trip back Emmaline thanked him for a fine day. "I had a good time Robert, thanks to you."

"I too," he said.

When Robert had them near the vast grassy spread he turned and warned her they would run to the barn. She held on tight. She became breathless and exhilarated all over again.

She never looked at her own summer home while running the horses as they passed by, so she didn't notice the small smoke escape from a chimney attached to the place.

Robert took the horses inside the barn and Emmaline went to the house to prep their last meal before leaving in the morning. They had a trip to take, an adventure to go on. Just being with Robert seemed like luck had come her way. She couldn't wait to go to Saint Augustine and then on down to meet her sister. Later they would venture over to visit with a man who invented things, lots of things. She felt like life was the river charging through her veins, she indeed felt alive! But first up tomorrow was a visit to a real European chateau. They'd been invited to stay for a couple days. She was likely to meet some very important people, educated and wealthy, not unlike herself, just older.

"No my Emmaline, you don't understand these people are the wealthiest in all of America," said Robert over dinner.

Emmaline had no reply but she was ready. Robert assured her she could pull it off, she'd impress anyone. He just knew it. He was most impressed himself.

That night Robert turned on the radio his dad had set up. He played some music for him and Emmaline to dance to. This was their last night alone. Somehow he managed to lift a bottle of champagne but decided to save it for a special occasion, like maybe when they found her sister.

Chapter 17

A day and a half later they arrived in Asheville and stepped off the train. The train still had full service as the strike which seemed eminent had not yet arrived. A driver from the Biltmore Estate loaded their luggage into his car. Another couple joined them on the trip to the estate. It was now late June and the countryside was green with the Smoky Mountains as a magnificent backdrop. The couple from New York City smiled in anticipation and in speaking with the other couple, apparently from Washington, D.C., this only heightened what they were about to see.

"Have you been here before?" she asked in a British accent. "Hello, I'm Rose."

"I'm Emmaline, and no, this is my first time to the Vanderbilt House," she said and extended her hand with the engagement ring on the fourth finger.

"Oh, you're going to love it. We are going to have

a marvelous time. They have hired musicians and artisans along with the cooks already living there. We are in for a rather delightful treat. How many days are you staying?"

"A few days, then we are off to the Florida coast. We'll be staying at the Ponce De Leon in Saint Augustine in fact. We are lucky to come and visit this fine estate while on our way south to Florida." Robert said.

"Forgive me for going on and on but I'm thrilled to be invited back. I attended their wedding back in '24, Cornelia's and John's and then came here for the magnificent reception. I never wanted to leave. You won't want to either," Rose said.

Rose looked at Emmaline as if to ask and how do you know them? Emmaline didn't miss an opportunity to expand someone else's vision. "My fiancé's father does business with a few of the invitees, you know the paper people and all their connections. We are so lucky to be coming in place of Mr. Charles Stephens and his wife Mary."

Done deal. There were no further questions.

Rose's husband George decided to enlighten the couple, who had never been there before, about the history. No one minded being informed.

"George Vanderbilt bought 125,000 acres in a beautiful setting near Asheville, North Carolina and proceeded to build his dream home. He modeled it after the elegant chateaus of Europe. Well you know, he had so much money from his father due to shipping and other entities, he had to spend it somehow. He loved art, too. The 255 room French Renaissance Chateau is both romantic and elegant set among the rolling mountains. It took five years to build and at one time had a hospital on the premises to care for the sick workers. Can you imagine that? Your own hospital?"

The group listened intently and asked an occasional question for which Rose was able to produce an answer, one that only a visitor would know having been there before.

By the time the couples reached the Biltmore Estate they were fully acquainted and looked equally forward to the approaching party in two days.

The yellow and silver 1929 Roosevelt, which looked like a Studebaker or Essex Sedan, turned right and pulled up to a gate. The guardsman nodded and waved him through. The couples were feeling impressed, finally they were going to meet the Vanderbilt's at their country estate. Emmaline couldn't wait to see the enormity of the chateau. Rose kept repeating 'you won't believe your eyes.' Robert was totally enthused himself. He gladly accepted his father's invite to go in his place. His father wanted him to write a short piece on the place that he would place in the social section. He told him he'd write it on the train and send it over the wire as soon as he made it to Saint Augustine, specifically the Ponce de Leon on King Street.

Emmaline warned him if he started writing pieces for his father it may become a habit and a profession, more so if he paid him. Robert told her extra money never hurt anyone and if they were to stay or return to Florida to pursue their dreams they just might need the cash. She replied to him that they would need more than a reporter's cash or salary if they were to open a real business or even a hotel. The argument was over before it even got going. They were young and really didn't know exactly what they were going to do. In essence, this was an exploration, an adventure.

"Look, look!" Rose exclaimed and they all turned to see where she pointed.

"Oh, my look at how large the place is. Extraordinaire." Robert's eyes were steadfast and fixed upon the exterior.

Emmaline took in the beauty as the car wound its way through a few trees and then drove straight up to the center. "Unbelievable. My how does one person, one family build such enormous home and so beautiful?"

"And it is modeled after places in Europe. Just think there is homes over there that have looked like this for many years. Incredible." Rose went on and on.

"So stately. I cannot wait to go inside and then look out the windows which overlook the rolling mountains," stated Emmaline.

"I'm supposing they have a large staff of butlers, cooks and nannies. How could anyone keep track of everything? I think it bigger than the White House!" Robert said in awe. He was more amazed the closer he became to the place. He squeezed Emmaline's hands and brought them to his lips and kissed them.

Emmaline smiled at the warm gesture and felt in awe, too. Somehow she didn't feel like she was in reality. "Anything that takes five years to build has got to be enormous and definitely worth seeing. But we get to be guests for a few days. I'm honored."

"Me, too," said Robert.

"As we are also," replied Rose.

The car drove through an entry where upon they could see a large barn for horses and carriages. Then they arrived and passed the front door. Emmaline kept focused as she saw several attendants come out to greet them. They retrieved their luggage from the trunk and sides and opened the doors on both sides for them to exit the car.

It was a warm day in June and the grass was green as were the rolling hillsides and the front smooth grass before them. One could see flowers over past the left of the large statuesque gables and windows. There appeared to be a large portico or sitting room open air style with vista views in every direction.

The couple in the car with them were greeted by a small child and baby with one guessed the couple who lived here. Introductions were made and then everyone was escorted to their rooms and told they would be given a small tour so they could find their way around the place over the next couple days.

"Did you bring your suit for swimming?" asked the lady with the baby in arms.

"Yes we did, thank you."

"If not we have some available in the dressing rooms. Please come in. We are so excited to have company. It's been a quiet winter and spring," she stated.

Robert was shown his room which was a couple doors away from Emmaline's. They unpacked their items from the suitcase, not the larger trunk both of them carried on this trip. Then they met in the hallway on the second floor and while they waited for the butler to return they sat down on a loveseat and decided what to do next.

Emmaline wanted to take the tour inside and

Robert wanted to go outside, but it didn't matter because they had all day. The party event was tomorrow starting at four o'clock. Fine attire, black tie if you have it, otherwise anything along those lines were acceptable the couples were told.

Emmaline became sidetracked thinking about her dress for tomorrow night. She and her mother had gone out shopping for her in New York and purchased a turquoise silk georgette dress with crepe style backing just passed the knees with pretty silver satin closed toed pumps adorned with a side catch. The dress had a silver beaded bow which cinched the waist slightly and rested on the left side. She was going to look fabulous!

In addition she had a couple strands of pearls to put around the neck and a sash for her hair. She'd put the sash on later in the night as she had a full rounded felt hat with feathers for a more dramatic look in the late afternoon. But when the dancing began she'd need the sash for her hair not the hat.

"What are you wearing tomorrow night Robert?"

"Surprise." He laughed. "No, I won't scare you. I bought a couple suits before I left. One is a summer suite, very light in color. You'll like that. I think I'll save that one for Florida. The other is a dark navy pin stripe suite with some new shoes. Hopefully, I won't get blisters from dancing."

"Go and put them on right now and wear them for the tour and outside. Break them in just a little," she instructed.

"Great idea, Mrs. Stephens."

"Mrs. Stephens," said the butler's assistant.

Emmaline looked up and explained. "Oh, I'm Emmaline Johnson, and someday I'll be Mrs. Stephens." She said and showed him the ring on her fourth finger of the right hand.

"Congratulations on the engagement. You've quite a lot to be looking forward to in your future. Are you on your way to visit relatives?" He asked politely.

She thought quickly. That sounds lovely. "Yes, we are on our way to visit family in Florida. They are quite excited." She didn't have an ounce of lying ability in her bones but this sounded like a wonderful answer to their escapade.

Robert returned.

"Mr. Stephens, congratulation on your engagement and all the best to you and your family visit in Florida." Emmaline winked at him and nodded.

"Why thank you kindly. We are fortunate to come here on our way to our final destination and family visit. How gracious of all of you here at the Vanderbilt Home."

"If you are ready, then follow me. We'll start up the stairs to reach the other levels and then finally down to the main level where we'll serve some tea and lemonade out on the side veranda.

Robert and Emmaline escorted one another up the stairs following the assistant Mr. John Edwards. He held onto the rail to balance himself and the couple wondered whether they should escort him and hold him up. But once they were at the top of the rounded staircase things went more smoothly. He explained about the electricity and plumbing and how lucky they were to be in on all those eccentricities which were becoming known as modernized adornments of late. He said everything was moving so fast the builder which was the father of the lovely daughter now in residence, kept up to date with the advancements of the time. He was a visionary and lover of the arts said Mr. Edwards.

The first floor proved to be the loveliest of them all and Emmaline and Robert adored several rooms down there. The library was Roberts's favorite, that and the side room for playing chess. Emmaline thought the banquet or dining room might be her favorite but then couldn't decide between the sunken and warm indoor solarium with several large ferns and sofas under a glass plated ceiling or the former. In the end she decided she liked the fern indoor garden. She and Robert took tea with some other visitors.

"How's the shoes, dear?" she asked.

"How kind of you to be concerned. They are fine, no problems. Shall we go and get some outdoor sunshine?'

"Perfect, yes."

The couple sat outside reflecting their lives and the summers spent in North Carolina. Funny, but these memories shared brought about many conversations and smiles. After a while they strolled out to see the flowers and gardens then walked arm in arm. Briefly, they stepped inside a greenhouse and went up and down the rows of plants, mostly garden like vegetables and delicate flowers. The weather was pleasant with a soft wind from the west. Later they took the steps inside and made their way to find a few moments of slumber before dinner.

They had dinner in the large banquet room even though it wasn't even half-filled. Rose told her that the lady of the house saw how much she loved the room and decided dinner would be in there. It was grand. Grand with two chandeliers, three fireplaces, thirty red velvet carved wooden chairs and five tapestries by an unknown English weave master. They portrayed 16th century work and tell of the love affair of Venus and Mars. Statues of Joan of

Arc and another, St. Louis, which reside above the entrance were done by Karl Bitter, a Viennese sculptor. This unknown arrived in the states in 1889.

Dinner was served and sixteen people were seated, friends and family and guests like Emmaline and Robert. How lucky were they?

An elderly woman named Edith asked Emmaline which room was her favorite.

"All of them," she stated. She felt her face flush. Emmaline realized she didn't like the whole table looking at her waiting for an answer. Then she said to correct herself, "Actually, madam, I believe I love the palm court as you call it. It makes me feel alive."

"Ah, yes, as do I feel alive in there as well. You should see what I do to it at Christmas time. Red ribbons adorn the place and I have trees decorated throughout the first floor. Snow falls on the window panes above and it looks most heavenly. Maybe you shall come back someday to visit at Christmas time. We'd love to have you both."

"Thank you madam. I shall remember your kindness," she spoke with manners.

After dinner the men were called to the library and Robert joined them. He found out quite a bit as they enjoyed an after dinner drink and a fine cigar. Baroque style details adorned the room that contained walnut wooden cases for a large volume of reads. Classic novels and works on art, history, architecture, and landscape gardening reflected the scholarly Mr. George Vanderbilt who could speak eight languages. The ceiling was an authentic painting by Giovanni Antonio Pellegrini (1675-1741) which Mr. Vanderbilt purchased from the Pisani Palace in Venice. Robert looked up at the painting and he was told the title, 'The Chariot of Aurora.'

He could see a winged man flying and a white horse held by Aurora he guessed with a chariot behind them. What did it all mean? He would have to look that up later here in the library. He hadn't studied these important works or Gods and Goddesses. It was so beautiful beyond words and on the ceiling at that. This intrigued him. This was the kind of thing that occurred in churches, not people's homes. Yet, this was not a home but an estate, a palace of sorts.

He decided that Mr. Vanderbilt was well traveled and moneyed. To select all these fine adornments must have taken him five years along with the construction. Amazing.

He knew he and Emmaline would have so much to discuss on the train trip to Florida. They would have to visit a library in Saint Augustine to answer any questions that might arise.

Chapter 18

Tea was served at two-thirty in the afternoon, earlier due to the late afternoon party. Mrs. Vanderbilt displayed the invitation which had gone out to a hundred and fifty guests including the house guests. *"A Night Under the Stars"* headlined the fine paper with times and dates and residence underneath. Someone had sketched a view out the large veranda window with the rolling hills in the background. Darkness had been added to give the appearance of a night with the stars above.

"How lovely. Did you make them yourself?" asked Emmaline.

"I did. One of the servants has an affinity for drawing and she helped as well. Good thing I discovered her hidden talent," she hinted.

Robert wanted to ask the question everyone present was dying to know. However, everyone remained courteous and obligingly denied themselves. Emmaline decided she was going to find out who this woman artist was by going downstairs later tonight.

What then began as a distant sound became apparent with police sirens and more than one at that.

"What is going on? Is there a fire?" asked the children's father.

Rose and John stood and walked quickly to the front door following the butler and servants. Mrs. Vanderbilt held her baby and went to the front window where she visualized five or more vehicles racing up to her front drive. They stopped and quickly exited the vehicles.

"What on earth was going on?" She said aloud to herself.

The policeman pulled out a paper and handed it to the butler which he quickly read and then handed it to Mrs. Vanderbilt's husband. He read the paper and began to explain with his hands and voice.

"Sir, yes we are having a party tonight but under no circumstances will we be breaking the law of Prohibition. We fully intend to be respectful of the laws of North Carolina as we have always done before."

"I don't want to have to come back here tonight and certainly don't want a catastrophe spread out in the morning papers. Do we have an understanding?" asked the officer.

"Why all the cars? Why come here at all?"

"There was talk in town and one thing led to another. It was advised we investigate, so here we are," instructed the officer. He had done as he was told and came out here to give a warning. "This is a courtesy call as you all are beloved by the city of Asheville. We wouldn't want anyone changing that attitude."

"Thank you for advising us and don't worry this is a dry estate. Hopefully, someday they'll put wine back on the menu but for now we happily oblige and obey the laws."

The officer instructed his men to return to their cars and off they were speeding out of the drive onto another call he supposed.

The men looked at one another. Well, half the night would be dry anyway. The whole country was boozing it up more than ever, especially in the south where moonshine was a way of life.

If people didn't make their own homemade wine, then they purchased liquor from distributors, which were plentiful. One was told that many police officers looked the other way. The men walked in feeling that courtesy call was a sounding alarm to be on their best behavior. And so they would until about midnight.

The guests finished tea and retired upstairs for a nap to freshen up for the big party. Emmaline thought *'A Night Under the Stars'* sounded perfect. The dress she was going to wear tonight shimmered and flowed. Her shoes were broken in so she could dance the night away. She hoped Roberts shoes would be comfortable and not bother him. She intended to dance with her makeshift fiancé in this fine and proper estate.

Downstairs was under a renaissance while the guests slept in the quiet afternoon near the end of June. Flowers were cut and brought in while food was prepared down below in the cooler rooms. There was going to be a nice feast with assorted meats, fruit preps, puddings, and breads. The staff would serve sarsaparilla and a fruit punch in a seriously large crystal bowl. Extra glasses were on hand as many guests these days in Prohibition brought their very own spirits with them. A gentlemen usually had more than one flask upon him which he shared with his own lady or several others. Discretion definitely inhabited many a person and his character especially in the south.

When Robert awoke he went to his window and looked out. He saw a Dixi burgundy BMW coming towards the estate. This must be the first guests to arrive. He'd better dress and go check on his fiancé.

Emmaline was just about ready when she heard a knock on her door. She answered the door and it was the couple from Washington, D.C. "Hello," she answered.

"Just making sure Emmaline that you haven't overslept. I would not want you to miss the party," said Rose. She was holding a gift elegantly wrapped in fine tissue paper with a bow. Emmaline spied the package and looked up at her.

"This? This is for the hostess which happens to be my friend. It's appropriate to bring the hostess a small gift for the party. But you know that, right?"

"Yes. I just haven't wrapped mine as yet. Actually, I forgot to buy the special paper. You know traveling so far and all."

"I'll send the butler up to assist you," she said.

"You know, I believe I will go down below and ask myself. I wouldn't want to detain Mr. John Edwards from his important duties today." Emmaline had no idea how she was recovering with these remarks today. Something was just right she felt. She felt good. She felt like she belonged here. Strange thought indeed. Nothing could be further from the truth.

Rose smiled and told her she would see her later. Quickly before many guests arrived Emmaline went to the basement and sought out the help with the artistic talent. She indeed helped her quickly then went about her work. Just as she had left, she returned to her room.

Another knock on her door and she knew this time it must be her date, her fiancé.

When she opened the door she caught a scent. It was delightful, something sweet she thought.

"Ready for the big event?" He asked her. He looked at her bed and it contained a present beautifully wrapped. "What's the package?"

"A hostess gift," she replied. "You know, it's the proper thing to do."

"It is. Oh, okay, perfect. Except where did you get a hostess gift?"

She looked at him. He looked back at her, perplexed.

"Sweetie our gift is the box of fine chocolates by Harry London."

"You mean the chocolate for Lilly?"

Emmaline bit her lip. "Yes, I do mean the very ones."

Silence.

"Robert, I will have to purchase another box when we get to the Ponce de Leon."

"But they may not have the Harry London select chocolates."

He was right. "I know. But this is what we have to do and I'll make it right. Chocolate is chocolate by the way," she retorted loudly but didn't mean to.

"Like moonshine, barrel whiskey and fine wine from France are all the same my dear. You of all people should know that they are not the same with a father that owned one of the leading bourbon businesses in America."

She glared at him in horror that he should bring up her dad. But he was right.

"There is a difference."

"I know." A chill ran down her arms and made her head quake and quiver.

"It's my fault for not thinking to buy a gift."

Chapter 19

As the couple descended the stairs they glanced out the windows and could see the lineup of cars. This was going to be one fancy party. At the bottom of the stairs the couple was greeted by John who escorted them to the dining room where they could place their gift and receive a drink. Follow the crowd was what John told them to do.

"Emmaline, you are looking beautiful tonight. The light blue color shimmers and is just adorable on you." One of the ladies spoke to her as they sipped their punch.

"Let's go look at all the decorations and flowers, shall we?" asked one of the others. The men mingled in the game room for a while when the ladies went browsing and admiring the details of the fine party.

"There is the dance floor set up for later tonight with the small orchestra over near the end wall. And look outside, the patio has garden wreaths and torches lining the encased area."

"Oh, I can't wait to dance outside tonight."

In the family dining room, not the large banquet room which was closed tonight, a violinist played his fiddle. Music flowed and pleasant scents drifted everywhere that Emmaline walked. Her date enjoyed himself playing billiards. He didn't know the gentleman but the man knew him. He knew he was Charles Stephens's son and he looked forward to meeting his old friend's apparent heir.

"I'm Ralph Heminger, pleased to finally meet you Robert. Your father told me about you and how he thinks you are very capable of finding your way, especially on this trip or adventure of yours."

"Thank you. Nice to meet you also. He told me about you as well. He said you had side by side businesses but you sold yours and moved south."

"Yes, I did. I work out of Tampa now. I understand that's where you are headed."

"Yes, among other cities as well, and I have my fiancé with me. We both have business, separate though, so we decided to travel and meet our goals, then return home."

Mr. Heminger lifted his eyes and he smiled just a little. "Well, I wish the both of you safe travels and a journey you'll remember for a long time. Maybe you'll return to live in Florida someday," he stated.

"Maybe. My fiancé is looking for a family member who has been displaced on the east coast. We'll do that first, then go down the west coast and visit Edison's lab and summer home in Fort Myers. I received a letter through my professor we were welcome to visit. Usually they head to the north in the summer but this year he's staying."

"I've been there myself, you know," said Ralph. "I prefer the bay in Tampa where I import goods for the needs of southerners, well, northerners too."

Mr. Heminger pulled out a couple cigars from his pocket and handed them to Robert. "Here, this is for you. I sell these."

Robert took the cigars, then insisted he couldn't possibly accept them.

"My present for you, the son of my dearest friend. I insist you take them both. They are a little moist yet, too soon to light. Wait about five days."

"Thank you."

"I've got more for tonight, later when the dancing begins." He laughed.

Robert laughed with him.

"What city you headed for next on this adventure?"

"Saint Augustine. In fact we leave tomorrow afternoon."

"Staying at the Ponce?"

"In fact, yes, sir. We will be there a few days before we connect with her family member."

"Beautiful hotel, recently built. Marvelous. Lots of entertainment over there on the east coast. The train station isn't too far, either."

"Sounds like we'll have a great time."

"More hotels are needed over there on the east coast with Flagler's train going all the way down. That's something you should think about doing. You're young, both of you could make that happen, build yourself a good business." He looked at him and wondered why he was lecturing this fine young man. "Sorry, I got carried away."

"Hey, that's mighty fine. My fiancé and I are looking for an adventure, something to be involved in and build. We just aren't sure as yet. Maybe this trip will help us to decide."

"You remind me of my son."

"Where is he? Far away?"

"No, he died a few years ago, got appendicitis and died during surgery." He breathed heavily. "Tragic, very tragic." He looked at him and instantly decided some humor was needed. "His mother died giving birth."

"I'm so sorry Mr. Heminger. Yes, tragic indeed. You've gone on though, and that is good. Your loss is immense almost too much for one to bear."

"Joking."

"I'm lucky to have both parents still alive. What?"

"I'm sorry. Dry humor. She's alive and run off with someone else. Now that's tragic for me. What else can I do but go on?"

"Mr. Heminger. I believe I'm not sure I can believe you."

They both started laughing out loud.

"Maybe we will decide to build something in Florida."

"If you do, contact me. I'd like to help be a part of your adventure. I would like to help you with that. Believe in me and promise me, you'll send me a telegram when you decide what it is you're going to do." He shook his hand and pardoned his leave.

Robert went to find his fiancé so he could eat dinner with her.

The sign he passed in the hallway said the dancing would begin at eight o'clock sharp!

Thankfully his shoes weren't tight and he would be able to keep up with Emmaline on the dance floor.

The gaiety seemed to increase as the night wore on. Hour by hour the laughter increased as did the music. It became louder and louder. The dancers did not wear out and only performed the Charleston 'one more time.'

Sometime around eleven after half the crowd had gone home the punch was revived. Glasses were poured and waiters carried them around to thirsty friends of the homeowners.

When it seemed like the party was just about over at eleven thirty the small crowd reveled and danced even harder. A toast was given to non-other than the fiancé and her partner from New York.

Rose lifted her glass and purported, "Let's toast to Emmaline and Robert from New York City. I think they traveled the farthest for this *'A Night Under the Stars.'*"

Glasses clinked and the party reignited spilling out onto the patio with the lit torches and flower clad green wreaths. "Dance, a dance for the happy couple!"

Emmaline and Robert held each other and danced right out onto the porch with glasses raised from onlookers, a mere encouragement for a splendid retreat under the stars.

The music didn't end but their dance did. They walked further away from the estate under the stars and found a concrete bench not too far away. They looked back and all the lights lit up the estate outlining the windows and beautiful drapery. One might think they were in a faraway land. Neither of them had been to Europe but they supposed this is what it might look like.

By the light of the house and some moon in the sky that neither of them saw they kissed. Emmaline felt faint, almost dizzy. She closed her eyes and let Robert hold her up with his arms stretched around her. He then held her head tight to his and kissed her like he had never kissed anyone in all his life.

When he finally let go she caught her breath but wanted more. And so Miss Emmaline Johnson, age nineteen and far away from home put her hands in his hair and brought him to her with a kiss as light as a feather yet connected for a lifetime. She felt love.

Later when they walked inside she searched out her new friend Rose. She found her and the two of them snuck out to the side veranda where Rose shared her cigarette with Emma. It was June of 1929 and Emmaline thought the timing was perfect to partake in the equality of smoking.

Robert and Rose's husband found the pair and brought them the prohibited. They brought them a glass of champagne with the bottle. Sounds from inside persisted for quite some time. "Blue skies," "Babyface," "Somebody Loves Me," "Singing in the Rain," "Charleston," and "It Had to Be You" played for them.

A friendly man claiming to be a photographer for the family came out onto the veranda with a man beside him. Pleasantly he asked, "May I take a picture for Mrs. Vanderbilt?"

"I suppose," replied Rose. Before they had time to pose or put down their drinks and cigarettes the flash of light went off and a picture was captured. Their eyes and vision a bit dimmed didn't see the man again. At this time of the night they could care less.

Later when the clock inside chimed three times all knew they'd had a wonderful time and now it was over.

The couples ascended the stairs, saying good night to a few late revelers. Once Rose and her husband had passed Robert and Emmaline he politely asked if he could spend the rest of the night with her. She looked at him and immediately responded, "But of course. We'll never be here again and I want that, that memory."

The couple slept late and was not disturbed.

As the car was being loaded with their luggage the couples were saying their goodbyes to each other. The elder lady Vanderbilt, Mrs. Edith Vanderbilt came out to say goodbye and wish the couples safe travels.

"Thank you kindly for traveling so far to spend time with Cornelia and her new family. I know she had a wonderful time. Please do come back again sometime."

"Your welcome Mrs. Vanderbilt," replied Emmaline before anyone else could speak up. "I had the most splendid time as did my fiancé Robert. We appreciate your kindness and hospitality."

Mrs. Vanderbilt nodded accordingly at the young woman. She was touched by her pursuit of finding her sister. After acknowledging Rose and her husband she turned to Emmaline and handed her a familiar package.

"Please accept this gift back for your sister on behalf of the servant who wrapped it for you and myself. My prayers are that you find her safe and well. Please let me know."

"Are you sure? I can buy more."

"Please take this. The servants want you to have it and so do I. She'll want those chocolates when you find her," said the fine lady.

She thanked her and the two ladies gave each other a brief hug. *That was sweet* thought Emmaline.

They left the 255 room French Renaissance Chateau and looked back through the windows of the burgundy Dixi BMW. "George Vanderbilt built one enormous place. I still can't believe we stayed there Miss Emmaline."

"I can't either Robert. I just can't."

Chapter 20

The couple departed the train and were immediately asked where they were headed.

"Seventy-four King Street," replied Robert.

"Over here, here's your ride."

The Spanish Renaissance Styled Ponce de Leon Hotel stood before them after they departed the quick trip from the train station. The dome, turrets and red tiled roof looked like a Spanish Mission or fortress in the grandest sense. They'd never seen anything like it.

"I love it. And we get to stay here. I cannot wait to see the inside."

Robert put his arm around Emmaline and she nodded her head down to his shoulder. She couldn't believe this adventure was bringing her more pleasure and excitement than she thought possible. They would even get to see Miss Pearl very soon.

Robert loved this traveling thing. All was

well, except they'd almost lost the chocolates for Emmaline's missing sister. But thanks to the kindness of Mrs. Vanderbilt she would get her gift. The couple had their rings on and from now on they were back to Mr. and Mrs., at least while at the hotel. After all the young couple had to save money in such a fancy place as this.

"Let's go inside," he said after the bellman took their luggage.

The place was lit up inside, every room had light.

Once inside their room on the fourth floor Robert set about making their final plans. *From here things would move along faster* he thought. Now their mission would be in full throttle.

He pulled out his leather cache bag and showed it to Emmaline for the very first time.

"What is this for? I like it, so gorgeous, I want it."

"This is where I keep my important papers, drawings, and possible inventions."

"Inventions?"

"Yes, Mrs. Stephens, there is more to me than what you think you know."

"I didn't know you were an inventor," she said intently.

"One must be discreet so one doesn't spill himself and have someone else take credit."

"Robert, really?"

"Yes."

"Can you even tell me what it is?"

"Not yet, but after Thomas Edison looks at it, an inventor himself, then I'll share with you. It will be verified or substantiated, hopefully, in the least."

Emmaline was curious, intrigued and not a bit dismayed. She went and gave him a big hug.

"Now listen close as we have many things to get done over the next two-three weeks."

"Do you think we can accomplish everything in that amount of time?"

"Yes, of course. Let's make the plan."

First up was to tour the hotel and grounds, then meet up with Pearl who worked here, somewhere. That they had to find out. She would give them further clues with a name of the man and the whereabouts of him who picked up Lilly and took her out of the orphanage before it burned down. His dad had said as much. Then they would make the trip via train and/or purchase a car to find her. The next part was not worked out. How would they get her out of her place without his permission? What if he turned on them? They had to figure out every possible scenario. Then back to the train junction to go to Tampa and down to Edison's place and back. It seemed almost impossible. *Maybe it was* he thought.

"We can do this, I know it," Emmaline hinted.

"I just want to be sure. I want to see if there is something I'm missing. Maybe Pearl will have all the information we need."

Emmaline smiled. "That would help us. Let's find her."

Robert checked at the desk. He inquired about a lady named Pearl, possibly, she was a cook he told them. The clerk checked the kitchen employees and found a lady named Pearl. He said she worked the breakfast shift in the kitchen and was already gone for the day.

They looked at one another and frowned slightly. "But, it says here she sometimes does extra shifts of cleaning and if one needed her to go to this address." He wrote down the address for them and they went off to find her but not before enjoying a brief tour.

The unmarried couple toured the hotel and enjoyed the palms which swayed outside. They seemed to be everywhere. It certainly added to the breeze seeing them sway and brush against themselves. They kept walking and found smaller streets to walk with artists and musicians everywhere. They asked someone if the street address was close by. It was. They walked a couple more blocks passing small houses and found an older wooden place with a small parking lot out front. It had a sign which read:

PEARLS FISH HOUSE

She not only worked the breakfast shift at the Ponce but had her own little fish house.

The sign said open 4-12 Tuesday through Saturday. It was Thursday and they wanted to leave on Sunday. He knocked and no one answered. He pulled out his time piece and read it. Three o'clock.

"Let's walk around back and look for a door to knock on. She won't mind, I just know it."

"What's that I won't mind about, ya say?" A voice from inside the screen door asked.

He recognized his Pearl's accent that of heavy Tropical Island flavor. "Is that you dear?"

"Yes, please da come in Mr. Robert from New York. I've missed ya," she replied.

She opened the door and allowed the couple to enter into her small, tidy place.

"I've missed you, too."

"And who dis is your mighty fine bride?" she

asked as she looked at her finger.

"I'm Emmaline!"

"Lee tell Emmaline, from de neigh bars Johnson family?"

"Yes, that's me," she said.

"Well nowa, you dis very beautiful. Tell mis Pearl why are you both just standing there in fronta me down here in dis Saint Augustine?"

"Long story. Have you got a bit of time?"

"Time? I altways have de time for me past. Sometimes it floats in on de boat and sometimes de train bringst it right to me doorstop."

They didn't know what to say to that. Silence.

"Sorry. Please, tis my pleasure to have ye both righta here. Come in. Come in!" She added. "This is ta mighty important. Serious, I'm taken it."

They explained their trip and how they hoped she could help.

She went over to her counter where the cash register was held and picked up a paper. It was todays and she slapped it down on the table. "Has you seen ta headlines yet?"

"No, we haven't. We just arrived. Now we are here."

Emmaline read the headlines, "Strike Hits July 1st."

"You might notta be going ta anywhere or not in

denny hurry, anyhow."

Robert breathed deeply and exhaled rather loudly that it filled the room with his frustration noise.

Emmaline swallowed hard.

Pearl just smiled. She had an earful for them.

Pearl told them to come back tonight as she wanted them to meet someone. She told them to come back around 7:30 for dinner and listen to some music entertainment later on. They left and promised to return. She said she would tell them all she knew tonight.

Meanwhile the couple strolled around the grounds of the hotel and decided on the short tour of the interior at three o'clock which was just prior to the beginning of their evening.

Emmaline and Robert learned of the millionaire Henry Flagler who built the hotel which was completed in 1888. It was a Spanish Renaissance design by a team named Carrere & Hastings. Exceptionally noted was Henry Flagler's friend, Thomas Edison, who installed electricity throughout the hotel. This was one of the first large buildings to have electricity and residents were not very brave as the hotel had to turn the power on and off for them when needed. Murals were by George Maynard who also later completed some for the Library of Congress. Mr. Flagler organized artists' studios out back and this attracted many up and coming artisans. The couple had seen some of these as they walked outside earlier towards Pearl's place.

The tour concluded with tea and lemonade on the covered veranda. Several others joined them and a gentleman by himself sat close by, his business unbeknownst to them.

"I think I like this Florida, Robert. Do you?"

"What do you like about it, Emmaline?" He asked. He was going to get it out of her.

"I dunno. It seems calm like time has slowed down. No one is in a hurry!" She proclaimed. *That's it* she thought. There's more time. Time stands still.

"No one is in a hurry because if they do hurry a long, they will begin to sweat," he said in retort.

"That's the obvious, yes, but think about it. You have more time and your day doesn't just skip by, gone forever." She looked at him and sipped her lemonade. She felt refreshed as a breeze came by and ruffled her linen top which further cooled her off.

"You have a good point Miss Emmaline. I suppose then much less is accomplished down here in your Tropics."

"But more relaxation and gazing upon these beautiful plants which grow to the sky. I could look at all this greenery all day," she said.

"Tomorrow we will go to the beach and swim in the ocean. You up for the game?"

"Can't wait to touch the warm salt water!"

"Great. Then let's get ready for Pearl's place," he said. "Garrett may want to join us tonight as he loves music. I'll ask him. He's always watching out for us anyhow."

Henry James Kelly smiled to himself as the young couple got up to leave and make way for their room at the Ponce de Leon. He lit his cigar and enjoyed the covered veranda amid the afternoon sunshine. He was onto a big story and they were the dessert. A deal is a deal and he planned to keep his part of it. His off white linen suit was cool and he removed his hat along with the jacket before he added some notes to his writing tablet. Henry kind of liked Florida himself just like the young girl did.

Chapter 21

Emmaline put her clothing items away and took a quick nap. The couple took aim to not infringe upon the other as their friendship or beginning love affair had not blossomed beyond a first kiss and special overnight at the Biltmore. They had plenty of time and both knew it. There was more of a fun element brewing for each of them. And don't forget Emmaline would remind them both. We are on a mission; we must stay focused for all of us.

Robert was feeling great about tonight as he would get to see his nanny and cook again. He had grown up with her in the house and was quite fond of her as she of him.

He had a surprise for Emmaline. He walked in before she got ready for the evening and handed her a gift bag. "This is for you. I want you to have something new from me."

She opened the package and pulled out a dress.

It was pale yellow with beads and jewels delicately placed in a special design. It was a piece of art she told him. The bottom had scallops and if she danced and twirled her legs would show a little bit.

"How fun. I can't wait to wear it. When shall I?" she asked.

"Wear it now, tonight. Pearl said there would be entertainment and I believe that means singing and dancing," he responded.

"Yes, I will. And I think I'll put that flower in my hair as well. That one over there that the maid service has left for us."

The couple walked in Pearl's Fish House and found a table. The place was half-filled and the entertainment had not yet begun. The stage was empty. A waiter came by and told them Pearl would be out shortly. When she did come out she was not empty handed.

"This is for you," said Pearl. She handed Emmaline a headdress made of beads and a plume of feathers. "One must look officially the part if one is to be a Flapper gal." She smiled.

Robert helped her remove the flower and place the headdress upon her head. "You look marvelous, so perfect."

"Great. Now what would you like for dinner? I do have a special, fish of the day with little pups, which includes dessert."

"I'll take it."

"Me, too."

"Parfect, I'll likely joint ya fer dinner n ketch ya up on de going's on `round tese parts n further on down to da south."

Pearl served them white fish with butter, stewed tomatoes with grits infused cornbread. Dessert was her very own banana pudding.

The conversation began after she served dessert. "I knows why ya all tar here."

"I figured maybe you did. Did my dad warn you that we were coming?"

"Well, tis a matta de fact yes. He is concerned fer yer safety."

"Safety? Why would we be in any danger?" asked Emmaline. She seriously had not given that a thought. What she had thought about was what if her sister didn't want to leave and come with her? Lately she blocked that thought. It was her own life. She may want nothing to do with her. But she did have to find out.

"Because tar is word tat de guy tat she married might be do un rum runnin n utter odd jobs."

"Rum running?"

"It's one thing for people to make their own wine and drink it in their homes but this Prohibition thing has gotten out of hand. Everybody wants a piece of the action and some people are willing to kill for it, the money that is." Robert said what he knew from his Dad's information.

"You don't think she's part of it do you?" asked Emmaline.

"Who knows what tee has ter doin? I have ta tell you what I heard him say, not even two months ago."

"Pearl, you saw him two months ago?" asked Emmaline.

"I most certainly did n he was braggin, braggin bout how tee got te girl outta de orphnage right before tee burned down. He said he was doubly lucky because now tee had de job doing somethin every te body vied fer."

"You think that is the liquor distribution business?" asked Robert.

"This is bigger than us. We'll need to call the police and let them handle it," replied Emmaline.

"That would be correct, Miss Emma, cept de police, some cops tat is are taken from de runners."

The two of them didn't know what to say. They sat there in silence.

"If you go getting in de middle of somethin one of ta could be hurt. I'm de very serious," Pearl said.

"What do we do?" asked Emmaline.

"Let me think Emmaline," said Robert. He wanted to help her. All she wanted was her sister, to talk with her and know her, maybe even help set her free.

"Dis guy, her husbin, goes further down to Mee ami ta deliva tis goods. He leaves her parently all ta lone fer long periods of time," said Pearl.

"How do you know all this?" asked Robert.

"Because I do. I want ya to discuss tis with me friend named Henry. You can trust him. Do as he says."

"Okay, when?"

"Late ta tonight, he be here. In da meantime, dance, dance n love da music. Me music gets started right taway." She looked over at the stage as the three piece band was setting up.

"Sure thing Pearl. We trust you, always."

After a couple of hits were played the couple got up to dance. The place was still about half full. Pearl's place usually got real busy at about ten and it was only nine o'clock.

Charleston's and other dances were strutted and twirled and sweated out. Mr. Henry James Kelly walked in about ten-thirty as instructed by Pearl yesterday when she met him. He was a friend of Charles Stephens, so he was her new friend, too. She would introduce the couple and set things in motion.

There was one person she would do anything for and it was Mr. Charles Stephens. He was the kindest and most honest man she ever knew. And she didn't know too many of those in her lifetime.

On a less than sultry night the couple sat outside on the back porch and listened to Mr. Henry James Kelly. He was making his case as they listened intently questioning one item after another.

"I contacted your dad when I saw the picture of you two in the society page," he said.

"The society page? Of what paper?" asked Robert.

"Yes, I'm sure you didn't think your picture would make the front page but it did. You were with Rose, a friend of the young Vanderbilt's, that's going to be front page in case you didn't know."

"Oh, I know the picture at two in the morning on the veranda when we ahem *cough* were celebrating the end of a beautiful evening," said Emmaline. "Oh, no!"

"Oh, yes." He said. "Don't worry, your cigarettes and drink were in the background. Only a seasoned, imaginative or nosy person might be able to tell what you were doing at whatever hour that was."

"All right, you have a picture. No big deal. So what?" asked Robert.

"The tag or caption stated your whereabouts

and that you were headed to Florida to visit a family member. Since Robert has no family members except Pearl down here, I figured you must be looking for someone else. So I called him."

"You called my father and asked him for what?"

"I asked him to let me do a story as I've been looking into the Miami distribution for a while. I know of its dangers and when I saw the picture of you two I couldn't help but want to assist and keep you from danger."

"You want to protect us. You want to help. Then you know who we're looking for, right?"

"Your father filled me in and I know about the fantasy marriage and the reasons for your trip. I hope you trust me. Your father believes in me and said it's a deal if I leave your names out of the story. We all win, I hope."

"Then you know I want to find my sister and ask her to come back with us and give us a chance. She might not want to I've been told. But I must try. I must."

"I can understand but I think you should let me talk to her first and not in his presence. He might be unruly or worse yet, downright villainous. He may choose to go down with the ship if he has a lot to lose. He's a kidnapper, a rapist, a rum runner, and probably a cheat, gambler, maybe even a murderer."

"He's right Emmaline. I cannot lose you. We are in this together and don't forget that is only part of the adventure. Remember my part, I must go down and meet with the inventor. He's waiting for us."

"Listen, here's the last part and I just found this out. The railroad is striking two days from now," said Henry James Kelly.

"We know. They won't have service aboard the train, no food or drinks or changes of linens," said Robert.

"Worse yet, sorry guys."

"What? Please tell us. What could be worse?"

"The train will not run from here to Miami for six weeks, there just isn't enough manpower. Your connections to Tampa and further south remain open."

Henry James Kelly lit his cigar. He was on top of his game. He rather liked this intrigue and variations in schedules. It kept him on his toes. It pleased him to no end. He had a couple who definitely needed him. He had a small story about sweet young love pretending to be married that he could let go by the wayside for Mother Nature to devour. But the big story was going to be his. He smiled.

"I'd say you best skip your plans of going to the ocean and head on down to Tampa and visit that white haired Edison while you have a chance. I hear he loves young talent and I suspect that is you." He flicked his cigar as Robert watched him enjoy the special treat from as far away as Cuba.

"I think you are right Mr. Kelly. We will leave in the morning. That okay with you Emmaline?"

"I have to trust this plan. It makes sense. You and I Robert get to continue and meet Mr. Edison and later, maybe, just maybe with a sweet little prayer I'll get to meet my sister Lilly."

"Sounds good."

"Oh, one more thing. You'll have to take the chocolates and give them to her from me. There in my room."

"Like I said sounds good."

Chapter 22

Emmaline and Robert packed and left the next day. When she couldn't find the investigative reporter named Kelly, she went and gave the package to Pearl who assured her she'd hand it off to him. She'd left a handwritten note for her sister as well. Mrs. Vanderbilt servants had wrapped her chocolates in very fancy wrapping paper so Emmaline didn't disturb that, she only added to it and put it in a paper bag for Henry James Kelly. She would miss out on the meeting but with lots of hope and luck, she'd get to meet Lilly on the return trip when they arrived back at the Ponce. Emmaline and Robert arrived in Tampa the next day and would only have a few hours to explore, just long enough to purchase a cigar and some food for the next leg of the trip. Robert saw the headlines, "Train Strike Hits East Coast."

"Well, no one is going anywhere fast except by

car," he cursed. "Let's hope the hell it doesn't hit the west coast."

Henry James Kelly had his own side kick, a helper or understudy, from his paper. He was a big guy studying literature and journalism in college. He was all his for the summer. The two of them left Saint Augustine for Miami with one side trip, to deliver the gift. He had an address from Pearl and a description of the place.

The reporters drove in the early morning hours, when the sun was high noon they found a few palm trees, parked the auto and ate lunch looking out over the ocean. The breeze cooled them off. Then it was back behind the wheel and off to find this little shack where a missing woman lived.

Somewhere between Okeechobee and the coast there was a road with a run-down wooden house on it. Why didn't it get blown away by the devastating Category Five Hurricane last year? He was telling his temporary partner about the mighty storm, adding that Florida gets hit with quite a few of these storms. "If you know one is coming it's best to leave and rather quickly. There's no sense in waiting it out. Mother Nature can win every time she wants to."

Following the directions as best he could, he turned right twice and finally a left. The area seemed to be deserted. There were no houses anywhere.

He did see a barn or two for storage he supposed. Most likely sharecroppers ruled this land but he saw nothing. He saw that many crops had been devastated. The land looked baron. Then he saw a tiny little wooden house and he turned down that path. It was out in the middle of nowhere to be sure. This had to be it.

He stopped the car far enough away as he didn't want to scare anyone. Henry walked around the car and came to the other side when he heard a cartridge click and load. He saw her with the rifle and it was loosely aimed at him. Oh Lord, he didn't need this.

"Ma'am, please. I'm unharmed. I'm not here to cause trouble. You okay?"

"Who are you?"

"I'm Henry."

"What does Henry want?"

"Henry wants to talk to someone," he responded.

"Who does Henry want to talk with?" she asked. Then she pointed the gun right at his head.

"Lilly, he wants to talk with Lilly. Is she here?" Henry asked politely.

Two small children came from around the corner and said, "Momma, he wants to talk with you." The two little ones, a boy and a girl, were dirty, disheveled and thin. Henry looked at them and sighed to himself.

The kids went to their momma and hung around her waist. Quietly, she asked them to go inside and they obeyed. The screen door slammed shut and she began again. "What does Henry want with Lilly? Answer me now!"

"Can we talk inside for a few minutes?" asked Henry.

"No we can't talk inside. Go ahead, talk."

"Is your husband home?"

"Why do you care?"

"I'd prefer we talk without him nearby. That is all."

"He's gone to work. What do you want? Hurry up, I'm making dinner."

"I have a delivery for you," Henry said.

"I don't take deliveries. My husband takes those. He'll be here tomorrow. You can deliver it then. Tomorrow." She turned to go inside and ushered them with her rifle to get in the car.

"I have a delivery for you, not him."

She stared for the longest time. She didn't know why except that she never received presents or deliveries. Maybe this was a trick to steal from what little she had. She'd remind David tomorrow that he needed to leave someone behind to protect her and the kids. Though, she doubted he'd listen. He never listened to her, ever.

"I have a gift for you from someone you've never met. Possibly, you don't remember as you were very young, maybe two or three years of age."

He had her attention. He didn't know for how long.

"I'm from New York. I don't know a soul from Florida except my two kids. Now, I think you better leave."

"You know Miss Lilly, sometimes in life somebody wants to do something nice for someone else. This is one of those times. I'd like to pass on a small gift from a lady named Emmaline. She's about two or three years younger than you and she kind of looks like you. She told me one day she would like to meet you, and until that day she wanted you to have this gift."

Lilly stood there once again frozen in time. The man walked to the car and retrieved a small brown bag. He opened the bag and presented her with a letter and a beautifully wrapped gift.

She eventually reached out for the gift and letter still holding the rifle in one hand. Her hands he noticed were filthy and callused.

"You work these fields?" he asked.

"Yes, I do. By myself mostly. You can buy some tomatoes, cabbage, or peppers. Do you want some?"

"Yes, I would like a couple tomatoes if you have

extra," he said. "How much?"

"Ten cents apiece," she said.

He pulled out a dollar and said to keep the change.

"Kids get me a couple tomatoes."

"Miss Lilly, please read the letter by yourself and don't let your husband see the gift. Please do me that favor."

She blinked. That was all she could do.

She held the present with the letter and waited for him to leave. No thank you, no goodbye was offered. Once she saw the car depart from the drive out onto the main road she went inside.

She tried to prevent the kids from seeing the gift but they'd already seen it. It was too late. She ushered them to go out and play while she made dinner. But instead she went to her room and closed the door.

She read the letter and not a single tear fell down her face. What was this woman saying? She couldn't believe the lies but why would she do this? What was this all about? She didn't care. She set the letter down and opened the gift.

Chocolates. She ate a couple, then a couple more. She'd give the kids some but then they'd tell their dad. What should she do? She must think about this. She went to the window. No car. Nobody.

Chapter 23

For twelve years she'd been in an orphanage in New York. It wasn't bad, but it wasn't good. No one ever came for her and picked her out of the bunch of kids. Every year twice a month many babies and kids got picked to go be with a family. But not her. They told her she was special so she got to stay there with the workers. She didn't think that was so special. After a while someone told her she was too old.

Then one day she was old enough. She became so excited, even at fifteen. She was told it was a single parent and she would finally have her family. They tricked her. After all this time they betrayed her. She was absolutely beside herself. How could they do this to her?

Standing in the door way was a man. He was going to be her family. This didn't seem right. This didn't seem fair. Where were the other children of the family?

She wanted to scream but no sound came out. Instead her stomach was kicked by a horse and she cringed and curled up into a ball. They found her lying on her bed in the orphanage. She was in pain. Pain on the inside that no one could see. She couldn't smile. She became catatonic for several hours. The paperwork was filled out in her despair.

She was led out with a small suitcase where her things had been dumped into. She couldn't say goodbye because she didn't want to go and she didn't want to stay.

Where was somebody who could hold her and say something nice?

That is all she remembered from the orphanage.

"Wait. I have a photo. Yes, where is that photo?" she said to herself.

Quickly, she tried to remember. She hid it from him because it held a memory that she had no answer for. She kept it stuck inside a drawer way in the back tucked in a groove. You had to take the drawer out. She knew he would never find it.

She found the old photo. It was a picture of her at about age two or three eating chocolates. She looked closer and closer until she could read the label on the box. Then she looked over at the box on her bed with four gone already.

"It's the same label. **It's Harry London! It's Hershey's!** How is this possible?"

"How is what possible momma?" asked her little girl.

"Oh sweetie. I don't know. I don't know what's possible? I'm scared."

"Don't be scared momma," said her little boy.

He came and gave her a big hug.

"Can we have a piece momma?"

"Certainly. Just don't tell your father. Don't tell him. I won't ever see you again if you tell him."

"Promise, momma. We promise. It's a secret, our secret."

Her little ones tried a piece of candy and then had a second. They began to fight over having a third piece when the pieces flew in the air and the bottom lifted out. Along with that a card fell out. Lilly picked it up rather quickly. All she could think of is one more lie that her kids would have to remember. He would find out and be furious. She might not live through this. Panicked, she yelled, "Quiet, mommy is thinking."

She opened the letter which had a letter P at the top. She read a note from another complete stranger verifying everything the first note stated. It was signed very simply with a woman's name, Pearl. Then she unfolded the money. Quickly, she counted it. It was five hundred dollars. What was going on?

She looked out the window again and began to panic. What would she do? What could she do? She had to make a plan and quick. There was no car and he would be home tomorrow. She knew her five year old boy, Jack, could do it. Could her three year old Ginny follow through? She began crying, sobbing so hard that her two little children came to comfort their mommy. Then she began to tell them of her plan and that it would happen tomorrow. She was sure they could do her this favor. She promised them more chocolates.

Lilly told them that tomorrow or the next day when daddy came home from work that she would ask him to have another driver take him to work as she needed to go to the doctor. It was urgent and they were expecting her at the office. She thought she was going to have another baby but she was having difficulties. She told them please don't tell daddy about the visitors or the candy as he wouldn't like it and he might even punish them for it. They promised.

Meanwhile, she set about preparing clothing, shoes, and food for her flight away while burning all traces of the chocolates. She hid the letter with her picture, money too. Tomorrow came and went. She never wanted him to return and now when she did, he didn't. Bastard she thought.

He and his cohort sat out on the front porch and drank for an hour before he even came in to say hello.

"What's for dinner?"

"Chicken soup."

"Chicken soup? Nothing else? Let me find something else around here." He looked high and low for something. He wasn't even sure what he was looking for.

"I can make some biscuits or potatoes for you both."

"That's more like it. Do it now."

"How's my creepers?"

She ignored him. He persisted. "I said, how's my creepers?"

"I need the car tomorrow to go to the doctor. It's an emergency."

"An emergency. What's the matter?"

"I'm having another baby and something's wrong. I know it."

"Well, dear, you should know. Fine, I'll have Luther drive me. We'll be gone for about a week this time. You'll be okay?"

"Yes, I'll be fine. The doctor will give me some medicine and I'll be good. I'll get some rest while you're gone."

"Kids have to stay with you."

"Yes, I know." It was just about over. She was almost in the clear. She breathed a quiet sigh of relief.

Then little Ginny walked in and said, "I'll miss you daddy."

"Miss me? Where are you going?"

"Nowhere." A quiet disturbance began and quickly subsided. "But you are. You are going to work tomorrow."

"Yes honey, like I always do. No need to miss me."

Lilly said a quick prayer. Tomorrow or the next day couldn't come soon enough. Here she was trusting complete strangers out in the middle of nowhere.

"Why is this place always a mess? Can't you even put away your toys? Why do I come back to this?"

"Hey Earl, have another drink with me. Forget about it."

"Hey, we should go to one of them clubs tomorrow night when we get down there."

The rum runners, Earl and Luther, passed out early and rose early just as well. They took Luther's car and never said goodbye. Just as well, this was a new day for Lilly.

She woke the kids, told them she wasn't having

a baby and not going to the doctor. Then she told them she found out she had more family, a sister, who was very nice and wanted to meet her. She wanted to meet Ginny and Jack, too.

"Really momma? We have more family?"

"Yes. I can't wait to meet them. I have so many questions."

"I can't wait either, momma!" exclaimed Jack.

Chapter 24

Earl and Luther drove in Luther's car which was nicer and newer than Earl's auto. They headed towards Miami. It would take much of the day. Usually, they had places to unload their stock all along the seaboard from Miami and up. But today was going to be filled with more pleasure, especially tonight. Luther knew just where to go. He knew where the money would be tonight. He'd been in this game since the beginning of Prohibition. He was trying to teach Earl the ropes but his younger prodigy was too greedy. He could tell when he stayed at his home last night.

"What you doing with all your earnings, boy?"

"What do you mean Luther?"

"You know damn well what I'm talking about. Your wife is practically starving and your kids, you call them creepers." Luther who had more scruples than Earl but still fancied in illegal activities, was questioning his involvement with Earl.

"I'm saving for my future. I'm going to get out of this business or take over the big guy. I'm not sure yet. I'm thinking about it. You want in?"

"Do I want in? I'm already in, you're not."

"What's that supposed to mean?"

"You haven't been here distributing for very long. They pay you pretty good and you have nothing to show for it. You can't even feed your kids Earl. You're a failure."

"Well, what do you have? Nothing. Why you doing this lousy work for someone else? Why aren't you running the show?"

"I don't have anybody else. You do."

"They're all right. I give `em what they need. They don't need anything else. I never had as much as them. Don't worry about them. They don't eat much besides."

Luther shakes his head and changes the subject but not before he thinks to himself how he ought to help that little lady out. It looked desperate at his place.

Ahead of them, already in Miami, at a little place near the beach were Henry James Kelly and his young reporter readying themselves for some casino betting. There was going to be some high stakes tonight they'd been told. 'Bolita' was a numbers game that had taken over the whole of Florida. Its derivatives were from Cuba. People liked it because it was fast and easy. Henry told his young partner he'd teach him the craps table and roulette wheels. The young man was eager and this venture he'd come on was much more than a study. He was having a good time and getting credit for it!

To get into a good game Henry was going to have to play during the day and earn himself a slot at the night table. While he played his partner rambled around on the beach and took in some sun and some sights.

At around seven the evening began. Earl and Luther arrived at about eight o'clock. They had a meeting with one of their bosses at eight thirty.

"You guys are being moved. There's some heat around here and the big guy wants us to move further south towards the Keys. There's more room for expansion down there. There's other players now," he instructed.

This meeting was taking place in a boat house just outside the beachside racquet club which was really a speakeasy joint and gambling off shoot. Inside the boathouse was a small room, an office type place with a few chairs and a sofa. On the wall hung a photo of a starlet, a real movie star and it was signed by her.

"Sure, no problem. We can do that. When?" asked Luther. Luther was in this business because his dad was in this business, only his dad died by gunshot. He had no other employment and just figured he'd do the time and then get away someday. That day had not come yet. Maybe next year.

"Where you sending us?" asked Earl.

"Further South, maybe Cuba. Just kidding. Key Largo I think it's called."

"When?" asked Luther.

"Two days. Come by and I'll give you the address then."

That was it. Just like that it was over here in Miami. Earl thought about what he was going to do. He sure wasn't taking his family. He didn't really want that burden anymore, anyway.

"Earl meet me in the club I have to make some arrangements," said Luther.

"Sure." Earl left and closed the door.

"What do you want Luther? The boss will do anything for you, you know that."

"I'm not sure about Earl. He has a family he doesn't care about and he wants to cut into somebody's business. He told me as such. Not sure who that is, though." Luther reflected what he'd been told. He didn't know himself who he might be after or what he wanted.

"We'll look into it."

Simple. Done. That's how it worked. He'd be gone to Key Largo in two days. He wasn't sure if Earl would be coming along.

Henry got himself a place at one of the evening's tables in a back room. Good for him. His game face, well, he was just another rich dude looking for women and fun. That's what he told them. He fit right in. His partner just watched and learned the tables.

Earl and Luther relaxed awhile with some roulette. Earl liked watching the wheel go round. This kept him from thinking about what he was going to do.

"I think tomorrow you better go back to that wife and kids. Take care of them Earl. That's what I think," said Luther.

"I don't care what you think. You see I'm gonna start my own place right here in Miami. I don't care about them. I know enough people on both sides; I'll play it both ways."

"You have to go back and tell her, give her some money to live on. Those are your kids, they depend on you. You've made a small fortune rum running for a few years now. Get out and find a new place. You owe it to them."

"I don't and I won't. But I do have to go back

and get a few things. I'll do that tomorrow."

"Two days from now we head to Key Largo. You have a few choices to make is how I see it. Do the right thing Earl."

Earl didn't know it because he just didn't pay much attention to details that didn't pertain to himself. He was being watched and not by the police.

Henry played his hands that night and came out a winner. He doubled his cash and earned some respect at the table. He knew he'd be invited back and that was what he aimed for. He wanted in on the inside. He wanted to know the players, to remember their names and occupations and nuances. This was what he was good at. That is why his bosses paid him so well. For a short while he almost forgot this was work. *What a job* he thought.

This little place had some midnight music sung by a beautiful blonde in a tight silky dress with high heels. She had her cigarette holder in place and kept the room at her pace. The entertainment was a bit of the islands right here on the beach in North Miami. Men and women perused the place after midnight and there wasn't an empty chair. Some danced, some played, some gambled but most swooned over each other.

Chapter 25

The mellow night and casual atmosphere did not last. Henry sensed an urgency when he visited the club the next morning. Yes, it was open before noon. He didn't see the duo he and his cohort had been loosely following. He inquired about Earl and Luther, as he had requested some supplies from them. One of the workers said Luther hadn't checked in yet but Earl had gone back home to gather a few items. He was moving out and heading south. Henry decided to wait this out and see if the Earl would move his family further south. He and his partner were heading back in two days anyway. He'd check on the place and the young wife with kids then. He was certain she would have changed her mind after reading the letter from her sister.

Henry figured he'd have it all wrapped up nice with a good outcome. He was prepared to transport all of them back north. He had hoped to telegram

Charles Stephens' son Robert and his friend Emmaline, the sister, in a couple days. They'd let him know when they would return to the Ponce so she could meet them there. Things seemed simple. They'd be returning from their quick trip down the west coast of Florida to visit the inventor.

Time for a cigar he thought. One of the workers tapped him on the shoulder before he had a chance to light his Cuban delight and told him somebody wanted to talk with him. He followed him out back and both stepped inside a boat house. There he presumed he would meet one of the guys in charge, or a big boss.

"Welcome to Miami! Glad you are visiting us. What can I help you with? You need some supplies? You opening a place down here?"

"Thank you. So many questions. I'm inquiring for one of my partners who would like to open a new hotel between here and north of here."

"I see. You want availability of resources for your future customers. Am I correct?"

"Absolutely, we are talking on the same level. Pure and simple, can you help me?"

"Tell me your time frame."

"Next year, the building is already in operation as in we are halfway done. Nine months tops."

"No problem. We can help you and it will be

discounted as you are a great card player. The big boss can attest to this."

"Sounds good."

"Great, we'll be in touch. Leave me the location."

"I'll drop that off before I depart tomorrow."

Henry James Kelly told his young partner the deal was on. All was set. They would be leaving tomorrow. "Too bad, Henry, I'm beginning to like it here."

"Well, then maybe you should put in for the new hotel right next to the newspaper building. You'd have both ventures knocked out."

"Great idea! Will you recommend me? I'll need your best review to get the position."

"Recommend you? I may join you."

"Then it's a done deal. Will request it as soon as we are back in D.C."

"We'll be checking in on that young lady on our way back to make sure she's okay. Maybe she's had some time to think about her future, the kids future or lack of it out there all by herself."

"Maybe we should head back there tonight or early morning as I heard them say Earl has left town. The guy probably went back to get his money." Henry's quick study was all over it. Henry nodded in approval, changing his mind from his earlier stance about waiting it out.

Chapter 26

Emmaline and Robert arrived at the home of Thomas Alva Edison and his wife Mina. They had been invited to tour his research laboratory through Robert's professor as Robert's field of study in college had been the study of horticulture and living things besides his business studies.

His professor felt that a visit here would encourage the young lad to pursue his true ventures in life, maybe giving him some direction with all his plans and ideas. Time would tell.

The couple was amazed especially at his laboratory and place near the water. It was very tranquil with not many people around. The Ford's place was right next door. That, of course, would be the builder of the Model 'T' and other vehicles, he explained to Emmaline. This would be quite an exciting trip. Robert couldn't wait to tour the lab as soon as possible.

First up, a quick look around the homestead, which one noticed a light bulb in each room at the center of the ceiling. Tonight when lit up it would be somewhat like a dream being in the home of the lightbulb inventor himself.

The butler escorted them across the street to visit with Mr. Edison as he was always in his lab from morning until lunchtime. Later he might nap for a while or visit his garden with Mrs. Edison.

On the way, there seemed to be small plants everywhere, pots and pots, and water bins, too. They followed the butler as he escorted them to the oversized wooden building. Once inside he took them to find Mr. Edison. Then he introduced them.

"Mr. Edison, I'm pleased to bring you these young travelers, Mr. Robert Stephens and his wife, Emmaline. They'll be staying with us for a couple nights and then returning to New York City after a stay at their summer home in North Carolina. You and his father met many years ago and recently his professor arranged for a tour and talk with the lad. He graduated recently and needs assistance in his future endeavors, employment and or business."

"Thank you kindly Jackson, you may return."

"Emmaline and Robert, thanks for coming all this way. Let me show you around."

"Thank you so kindly. What a large place you

have here and certainly congratulations on all your inventions. However did you come up with all those ideas?" Robert was practically shaking in the presence of this fine gentlemen. He couldn't be more pleased.

"Oh, don't fuss on me. Brag to my wife tonight over dinner. That will make her feel good for all the absenteeism on my part. She married a tinkerer. God bless her."

"We will be pleased to extend our appreciation," issued Emmaline, ever so quietly.

He led them around and showed them what he was working on. So many things to see. Robert became even more excited as he couldn't wait to show him his sketches.

"We will look at those tomorrow afternoon on the back porch. It faces the Oceanside and it's a wonderful place for inspiration."

After a while he told them they could return to the home across the road and he would join them for dinner.

Robert held Emmaline's hand all the way back to the homestead across the road. They went inside to prepare for dinner and offered any assistance from them if needed. Mrs. Edison said for them to go and read before dinner. "Just relax."

Dinner was held late and Robert sort of figured

out that that was for the overhead light fixture to get the full recognition. Yes, it did just that and Edison explained to all of them how he came to produce that light bulb, that fixture on the ceiling. He was very proud of that and later so many more things came to him as he tinkered in his lab up north and here. Robert and Emmaline listened and listened until they were filled with inspiration.

"I cannot imagine making so many items for everyone to use. You are brilliant and will be remembered forever. Thank you for entertaining us in your home and allowing me to see where you work. It pleases me to no end."

"Thanks for coming. It was a long trip. I hope you are inspired and will help the world with inventions of your own." Mr. Edison was so polite.

"Tomorrow, we'll look over your sketches on the back porch and then the two of you can take a row out onto the bay or ocean. Mrs. Edison will have the cook prepare a small party tomorrow night so you can meet a few others who have helped me and I them."

"Yes, we would love to take a row out on the water. Sounds lovely. Tomorrow." Emmaline was already planning what she was going to wear. She had purchased three pretty dresses in Tampa one of them would be perfect. The French light-pink satin, sleeveless and scalloped short dress would be perfect for the boat. She would save the other two, a vaudeville red and black beaded dress and a Japanese styled new-green with coral and bird cages stitched pattern for another time.

Thomas Edison and Robert Stephens became familiar with one another the next afternoon on the porch. Robert was still closed with his sketches towards others but did want the inventor himself to eye the various drawings. They looked and they looked and Mr. Edison gave him his opinions and encouragement.

Emmaline served them fresh lemonade and blueberry scone biscuits she had made herself. "I made these. I hope you enjoy them."

"Thank you. I'm sure we will, especially since you made them." He was teasing her and there was quite a lot of playfulness in there as well. She smiled and he winked at her. So did Mr. Edison. He just thought them a young couple in love. No, not in love yet. But happening at the very moment, quite possibly right over a serving of lemonade and blueberry scones.

"Don't forget the honey, Emmaline," asserted Mrs. Edison from the back of the kitchen area.

"Let me get the honey, be right back." She excused herself and came back instantly with a small jar of honey. Butter, too.

"I don't know what you will be doing sweetie but your husband has many ideas and plans. What is it that you want to do?"

She paused and swallowed and tried to think of herself. "What?"

Silence.

"Oh, yes. I know. I want to open a hotel." And with that she turned and did not wait for a response.

Robert didn't know what to say. He just hadn't expected her to say anything like that.

"He himself swallowed and cleared his throat, "I believe we will be opening a hotel and maybe with a small lab in the back or a room to try my inventions."

"You better go for that row on the bay while it's still calm. Do you know how to row a boat?"

"Yes, I do. I learned when I was a little boy up in New York at a lake."

"Perfect."

Emmaline appeared out by the dock and joined Robert. She was a pink mist and shimmered when she moved. The only thing that Robert could think about right now was kissing his beautiful Emmaline. Mrs. Edison had given her a telegram that had just arrived. The couple boarded the small boat with oars and undid the lines attached. Off they went rowing out to sea.

"Tell me when you want me to read you the

telegram." She wanted to get this out of the way.

"Okay, go ahead." He wanted this over with also.

"It says it's from your father, Mr. Stephens of New York City. What do you suppose would be so urgent anyway?"

"I don't know. It can't be good because he would just tell me the good stuff when we meet in North Carolina later this summer."

She tore it open and looked for the message. It was rather long and detailed.

Chapter 27

Robert watched Emmaline's lips move when she began reading the telegram. Immediately though he stopped rowing after the first sentence.

Robert and Emmaline

I'm happy you made it to Fort Myers to meet with Mr. Edison. How delightful. What does he think of your plans? Your inventions? I'm sure he's as excited as you are to meet with such a bright young fellow. You probably are aware of the train strike down the eastern seaboard to Miami. My reporter friend from D.C. has just pressed me a report and I'm pleased that you allowed him to go find Emmaline's sister. It is better that way, so you both are not in harm's way. He reported that he was able to meet with her and give her the gift and letter. He will stop by there tomorrow and make sure that she knows she can meet you back at the Ponce. Telegram me when you'll be there and I'll let them know. Regards to

Emmaline!

Your father,

Charles Stephens

"Oh, wonderful!" Emmaline screamed. "It might really happen. I'm so excited, Robert."

"We must telegram father when we'll be back there at the Ponce." Robert exclaimed.

"Yes, we'll do that."

"Emmaline, they are alive. The reporter found them, alive. He spoke with her and is going to get them tomorrow. Trust me. I have a hunch about this."

"Robert, I surely hope so. I want to believe. What possibly could go wrong?"

"Emmaline, I know you have faith. I know you believe in good, that things happen for a reason and goodness prevails. That is why we made this trip in the first place."

She eyed him longingly and then closed her eyes for a moment. Here she was on a boat out on the bay in the Tropics and he was asking her to have faith and believe. She leaned forward as did he while they kissed softly as tears fell from her eyes.

He wiped away her tears and whispered to her, "I love you. I love you."

She kissed him again and told him back, "I love you, too."

Robert shook Mr. Edison's hand and thanked him for allowing Emmaline and himself the visit and tour.

"You're welcome. Please come back. Though, this is likely the last summer we'll ever be here. You'll have to come back in the winter, I suspect."

"Thank you kindly. We'll definitely stop be if ever down south again," said Emmaline politely.

Quietly and away from the ladies he said, "I like that idea of a walk in cigar room with the right climate. Humidity. You could sell many cigars and they would last longer, be fresher, I suspect. That's the best idea you have, and oh yeah, the lightweight shoes is good, too. Work on those, let me know how I can help."

"Thanks. I will." Robert smiled and felt relieved that someone of his importance and knowledge liked some of his ideas. The cigar idea of his was only a recent one since arriving in Florida. He had at least a hundred drawings in his portfolio of ideas he'd been working on for three years."

"Only one way to find out if they'll work is to try them out my young man."

Looking back at the lovely white wooden house adorned by green shudders, an orange tiled roof, with a surrounding porch they smiled. Hard to believe they came all this way to meet someone. It was inspiring, though. Large plants were on both sides of the front porch and Mrs. Edison had called those *'Traveler's Palms'* as they offered fresh rainwater to traveler's. Emmaline thought she liked those best of all. The plant transported anyone back in time or forward as people always come and go.

"I want to have those at my hotel someday."

"What's that Emmaline?"

"Traveler's Palms," she said and pointed at the tall palmed plant so Robert could see.

He put his arm around his lovely friend and kissed her head on the side. Back to reality he thought. Let's make it good.

With that the couple was off to the train to get back up north. Robert was feeling rather satisfied but Emmaline couldn't help feeling worried. They would go back and forth for the next few days as an uneven accompaniment.

The couple loaded up with supplies as the train had no service. It was not filled either. Plenty of rooms were empty and the dining room was sparse of patrons.

Chapter 28

Henry and his understudy set out very early and traveled back up north. First they stopped at the small wooden house out in the middle of nowhere near Okeechobee. He hoped to find the girl named Lilly and bring her and her kids with them back to the Ponce to meet up with her sister. He had a plan to divert Earl and get them out safe. If she didn't want to go, well, then that was her choice. She was old enough to be on her own. The sun had barely escaped over the horizon. Dusk. It was quiet, the birds weren't even awake as yet.

Their vehicle was the only car on the road. Peaceful. Henry smiled. He was going to do a good deed today. As much as he liked work, this was enough better. If he wasn't a decent man he thought he might like to knock off the bastard himself. Well, he would hurt him or slow him down just a little.

He pulled onto the dirt path and the house was

visible, and so was the police car.

"Oh no!"

"What?"

"Wake up," Henry said. He nudged his partner. "Get the gun out, just in case."

He handed it to Henry. Henry slowed the vehicle. He wasn't sure what he was headed into.

Henry's heart quickened. His palm became sweaty on the slick driver's wheel. This wasn't in the plan. He spotted a policeman walking about looking for something.

"What's going on?"

"Look around. See if you spot any other vehicles?" Henry instructed. "After I talk with the policeman you keep him busy while I look around. Keep him occupied with questions and thoughts about what happened. You got it?"

"Got it."

"We got a notice that there was a shootout an hour or so ago. We've found four dead men. One had a rifle and the three others hadn't pulled their guns out yet but their car was loaded with weapons. Have a look. Unbelievable. They were ready for a shootout but somebody caught them by surprise. And I don't think it was the fella with the rifle. We'll see."

Henry didn't know what to say. He presented his

reporter's badge and identification.

"Where were you and why are you here?"

"Oh, we were passing through and heard the sirens going off. Came out to check on things. Anybody else live here?" Henry gave him his best answer on the spot.

"Nobody else so far, but it does look like kids live here. There's a few toys out back, cooking utensils inside, etc."

"You alone?"

"Yeah. We're short today. I'll have to fill this out and call for a hearse later.

"Can I have a look at the dead guys?"

"Sure, I don't see a problem with that. Let me know what you think happened. Don't go getting sick on me or nothing."

Henry went around and looked at the faces of the dead and recognized a couple of them from the joint on the beach. None of the guys he played cards with. Then there was Earl with a splattering of holes across his chest. No heartbeats left there. He should have listened to Luther instead of trying to outdo the big boys. Now he lost everything. Except where was his money? Luther said he'd been saving it somewhere out of sight from his wife Lilly. Lilly, where's Lilly? He hoped to God she wasn't here dead too or the kids. He felt sick all right when he thought about them.

Henry excused himself for a moment and went to his young friend. "He's dead. But where do you think a guy would hide money from his wife and save it for himself?"

"You're asking me, what have I learned in school or at the office?"

"Yes, where does one hide the money? You tell me."

"Either on them, like their car, or in a safe place that only they go to like a barn or outhouse, etc."

Henry looked around. This was a crime scene now but he knew that the wife needed money, and hopefully, she was still alive. Think quickly. Luther's car was here but not Earl's. Strange. "Keep talking with the officer's while I check out the small shed."

His partner occupied the officer's asking about details, identification of bodies while Henry went to the shed.

He knew Earl wasn't too smart but would hide it where she wouldn't find it. It must be in the tools but not the garden kind. He looked around where the big shovels were kept stacked up against the wall and saw a small loft area. He smiled. It had to be up there.

This wasn't the sort of thing Henry did on a regular basis. Absolutely not. He just remembered those kids and the line of work Earl was in, if he didn't do this now nobody would give anything to those kids, ever.

"I think we've got everything here. I'm about done. I'll check the deeds in town as to who owned this shack."

"Good luck officer."

Henry returned and nodded to his partner.

"Let's go Henry. We are headed home. Good luck officer. Looks like all you need is right here. They killed each other, I suspect, probably over a gambling debt for the farm."

The officer hadn't thought about a gambling debt. It did look straight out like a shoot-out. Probably anger over something, maybe farming, maybe not. Gambling? The officer would be thinking about that one the rest of the day. That reporter was probably right.

Henry hid the loot in his own auto out of sight. How would he find the girl named Lilly? He hoped someone didn't take her and the kids. Earl's car was missing. Was that a good sign or not? She'd told him about Earl's car, what color and type it was.

As soon as he got to the next town he sent a telegram to Charles Stephens. He wished he had better news but it wasn't all bad.

Chapter 29

Lilly stepped off the train with little luggage and her two small children. Bright eyed and well rested she set down foot in North Carolina. She'd never been there except to pass through. She wore a hat and a new dress that she'd purchased on a stop off the train in Saint Augustine. She'd met with Pearl and was following the letter explicitly. What harm would it be to follow someone's advice other than Earl's which was only to his benefit anyway? She'd grown very tired of the man who essentially kidnapped her more than six years ago. Would he come after her and the kids? She decided that he would not. Pearl assured her that he would not. She'd read it in the paper the day Lilly arrived with her kids. He was dead. It was over. She was not sad nor glad.

Now someone wanted to meet her through a box of candy, chocolates just like in the photo she was eating at age two or three, she might just get to meet family. The letter said she had a sister named Emmaline who was younger by a couple years. Pearl told her the story sounded unbelievable but it was worth trusting.

After all, the picture proved the lady knew what she was talking about. At first Lilly was mad, angry that she had no family and why would anyone want to come and disturb her now. *Leave me alone* was her first thought, then she warmed to the idea of getting away from Mr. Creeper himself, who was all about himself anyway. Lilly suspected he was keeping money from them when they went on a double date with Luther's girlfriend. The lady actually asked her how she spent all the money the two of them made. Lilly just replied she bought food for her kids, farm and garden supplies, sometimes clothes, too.

"You're missing out on something because Luther has bought me a house on the ocean and we have three cars and ..." the lady went on and on.

The letter said to call this number, one of the hired hands would come get her and bring her back to meet Emmaline. Sure enough everything was working out like the letter and Miss Pearl stated. She waited and they'd be there to get her this afternoon. Lilly glanced at the newspaper outside the storefront window.

Ginny and Jack hung close to their mom and climbed into the car when it arrived for them. They didn't have much luggage, except a few small pieces.

"I'm Deuce and this here is Francis. You are Lilly?"

"I am. This is Ginny and Jack," she said not knowing what else to say.

"This is going to be a surprise for everyone! We have decided not to tell them of your arrival. They'll find out as soon as they arrive, which should be in about a week or less."

"Thank you."

"We know you must be curious. We'll show you around the place and you can settle in before they arrive."

"Okay, sounds good. Maybe I can help with the cooking or something," Lilly offered.

"That would be mighty fine, yes."

"There's plenty for the kids to do too. There's a barn with chickens and even a big swimming lake. Emmaline will take you there after she arrives."

Lilly listened to all the conversation and then dozed off as the sound of the auto put her to sleep. She didn't have to worry about her kids as they fell asleep and were contained in the auto. No one could harm them now. She felt safe. She fell asleep. She began to dream.

She began to dream about the last few days she'd been traveling. She'd left quick and never looked back. She didn't ever want to see that place again. In Saint Augustine she stayed at the Ponce de Leon after purchasing new clothes with Pearl's help. They all had cleaned up and slept very well. Pearl assured her that where she was going was the right place for her. It had been Pearl's money. She wanted to give it back or pay her back but Pearl insisted she help someone else someday when she could. She told her she wouldn't tell anyone that she and the kids had been here.

"Ta meal is on me," said Pearl. "You art going te love Miss Emmie line. You look jus like her, let me say. Windersful kids, too. Bae good fer yer momma now," Pearl instructed.

"Thank you," said Lilly. She didn't know what else to say. Why was she so kind? Some people how did they ever become so kind? She didn't know.

That first night after she'd left there were parties everywhere. They were celebrating the Fourth of July, Americas Birthday. This was something the kids had never seen out in the middle of nowhere. They had been to a picnic but never seen lots of folks celebrating all day and night long. They looked out their hotel window and could see fireworks off in the distant.

Pearl was the one to arrange the men who picked her up. She called them and instructed them when and where. She told Lilly about the summer homes and there was plenty of room for her to figure out her next step. She told her don't worry about a thing. They have been looking for you for a long time.

Really? A long time, well, why didn't they find her sooner? That thought still upset her, over and over, every time she thought about it.

"Must not think about it," she said out loud.

"What did you say?" asked Duece.

"Oh nothing, I'm just waking up."

Francis looked back at the lady in the back seat. She looked worn and torn and tired. Her skin was translucent and pale and she probably hadn't eaten right for a long time.

"You're mighty thin Ms. Lilly. Are you sick?" He just came out with it.

She looked back at him. He had a nice sincere smile. What should she tell him?

"Francis, right?" He blinked his eyes meaning yes. "Things have not been right for some time now. I'm sure of it as you all are treating me very sweetly."

He smiled. She smiled back and began to cry. He handed her his kerchief to dry her tears. One more sweet and tender gesture. Lilly couldn't take it anymore and wept.

Her kids woke and remained glued to their mother's side. She looked out the window.

"Almost there," was all he said and pulled into the drive that ended at two large summer homes.

"Summer homes," she whispered.

"Miss Lilly, you don't know this family yet but they are very nice people. I think you'll like it here by just being around them. Please give them a chance."

"Which home are we to stay in?" asked Lilly.

"There's only one open right now, until late July, when the other family is coming to stay. This one over here is where you'll stay. Unpack your items and then join us for dinner. We'll explain where everything is and what you'll want to do."

Frances took her luggage and showed them to their room. He figured the kids would want to be with her for a while. "This here is your room with three beds and a large spot for a few toys."

"We don't have but one toy. There was no room for much to bring," she said.

"I figured you wouldn't have brought much with little room traveling, so we accommodated here from the lower level. The kids used to play here all the time. Mostly Robert went next door but he always wanted to make sure he had toys for when his best friends came knocking, all three of them."

"Ginny and Jack will love it. Thank you again."

Teddy bears, toy guns, stuffed animals, a scooter, cars, trucks, a wagon, toy airplanes, a very large dollhouse, a tractor, a chemistry set, a furry bunny, and Lincoln logs. Ginny and Jack looked at their mom and back at each other. "Go ahead, find something to play with. Be careful and don't break anything. Promise."

"Promise, mother," said Jack. They looked like they'd seen a ghost! Eyes so big, their mother thought they'd be playing marbles soon. She joked to Francis.

He responded, "Nothing like a kid who's never had a thing." He said it and then wanted to take it back and say sorry. He'd put his foot in his mouth his mother always told him he was brutally honest. To this day her words had never been more right than now.

Ginny brought her mother several books sitting on a table. "Momma, can you read these to me?" she begged.

Her mother looked at the titles, 'Winnie the Pooh, Dr. Doolittle, To the Lighthouse, and The Velveteen Rabbit. She said, "I will teach you to read to me."

Ginny began looking at the pictures and turning pages. She was enthralled.

The one thing she remembered about her first fifteen years is that she taught herself to read.

The five of them enjoyed dinner that night especially the two hired hands who hadn't had company for over a month now. The children ate voraciously. Lilly enjoyed the company and later the solitude. Her children played in the bedroom while she read a book herself. It was quite peaceful. She still felt like running away the best option. She would soon find out everything. Very soon.

Chapter 30

On the third day Francis knocked on Lilly's door and said breakfast would be served soon. He told her to dress as someone wanted to meet with her. Someone from the family he told her. The last couple of days had been sweet and very smooth like for all of them. She wondered if Emmaline had arrived early. Francis had told her she would likely arrive on Friday.

She put the dress on she had worn via the train as it was her best. She had her children dress in the newest item she'd purchased for them. She still had 400 dollars left. She wanted it to last a long time.

She held Jack's hand and walked down the steps. His big sister trailed behind them. They walked into the dining room as Francis and Deuce had been serving them their meals there for the last two days. Sitting at the table reading a paper was an elder gentlemen with glasses on. He was medium build with graying black hair.

"Hello, Miss Lilly. I am happy you have arrived at our homes. I wanted to come by earlier but felt you needed some time to adjust to the new surroundings."

"Yes, thank you. We have adjusted and relaxed up in the room above. It is quite comfortable." She didn't know who this was. Should she ask or wait until he states his name?

Francis spoke up when he saw that she became uncomfortable. "Miss Lilly, this is Emmaline's father, Mr. Jack Johnson."

"How nice to meet you Mr. Johnson. I have yet to meet Emmaline, though. I'm told she is coming in a couple days, maybe even tomorrow."

"Forgive me, my manners lack as I've been alone now for quite some time." He stood up and went to greet her properly. He shook her hand.

She stared at him and nothing clicked. She didn't put it altogether. She was flustered and confused. "I'm sorry, I'm confused. Why are you here and not with your family?"

"That is a very long story and I think we should have some morning tea to discuss this at length. Maybe the children would like to eat in the kitchen with Deuce and Francis, so we could have privacy."

"Yes, I'd like that." She maneuvered to the

table, set with fine linens purchased from Ireland. The porcelain china was gold lined, scalloped, and belonged at an elegant hotel in France.

Deuce served them tea and replied, "I'll come back with breakfast after I feed the children."

"Thank you Deuce, sounds good. Where do I start Lilly? I have so much to say and little words that will do any good at this point." She could see him struggling. It must be important she thought.

"Please start anywhere. Just begin. I only know what two short letters told me. It's a good thing my husband didn't see them or I don't think I'd be here right now."

"Yes, two letters? I know of Emmaline's help. There was another?"

"At a moment's notice I changed my life. I can show you the letters. Someone named Pearl gave me money, too. I'm not sure what I'll be doing but I came all this way. So please tell me everything." If she could just come out with it, then he could to. She waited and looked at him right in the eyes. She waited.

"Miss Lilly, I made a terrible mistake that I must live with for the rest of my life. My dear wife has forgiven me but I cannot forget. I have lost her respect and most of her love. I know it."

"I'm listening." She turned her head in disgust,

not at him, but at the utter lack of respect she felt for most people.

"A long time ago, I tried to help her. I thought she needed help but she didn't. She just needed a shoulder to cry upon or ears which would listen. But I went and tried to take care of matters. I went to an orphanage and came home with a baby for her. She had lost a baby of ours and I wanted to stop her from crying."

She waited.

"After we adopted the baby from the orphanage, I told her I left a sister there."

She winced. She waited. She longed for something she didn't know what.

"I couldn't or wouldn't adopt both of you and I was sure someone would come along for you. You were beautiful and smart."

She swallowed. It hurt.

"My wife got over it in front of me, but I knew she thought about you every time she looked at the baby. She named our next child after you. Her name is Lilly."

She felt light. She wanted to faint. She wondered. Now she knew.

"Lilly," she said barely audible. Lilly felt nauseous and light. Then her head felt the room spin and she fainted. She fell over to the next chair.

Mr. Johnson got up quickly and went to her. He took a napkin and wetted it in the glass of water next to her. He patted her forehead and lightly slapped her cheek. *She was pale, paler than a few moments ago* he thought.

"Lilly, wake up dear," he said.

She began to come around and opened her eyes to find herself staring at this man.

"You'll be okay. How do you feel?"

"I don't know. What happened?" she asked. She stared at the man in front of her.

"Dear, you fainted at my words. I'm so sorry. Truly I am."

She wondered what to do? What to say?

"Here take a sip of water and I'll have them bring the food in shortly."

"What are you sorry for?"

"Please."

"I ask you… what are you sorry for? Are you sorry you left me behind? Are you sorry you adopted Lilly or that you acted cowardly?" Her bravado was killing him.

"I was a coward for not thinking of your life."

He said it. That was as plain as day, as dry as rice, like salt on an open wound.

"You also didn't think of your wife's life, letting her be a mother to a baby who had a sister. How unfair to Emmaline."

"Once again, you are right." He lowered his head. He lost his spirit in front of her. "Why didn't you kick me then right there in the orphanage? I wish you would have. I most certainly deserved it."

"You probably are no better than Earl. But he's dead."

He looked at her with distaste, the vile in him enlarging. How dare she take him down when he's trying to absolve himself of his devious deed?

"We are just human. People do insane things like go to an orphanage and pick out a bride."

She stunned him. He looked at her. No, that couldn't have happened and all because of him. He didn't know that.

He stood and left her side. He walked to the window he slapped his forehead, then put his hand in his pant pockets and jingled a few coins. They both heard it.

"I don't want money."

"Of course, you don't. You didn't come this far to take anything. You came to find, to share family, and maybe love. That is what you deserve now, and deserved then!"

She stared at him once again. She didn't love him, she didn't know love except that of a child.

"I will do anything for you. That is why I'm still

here and I know it."

"What is that supposed to mean?"

"You don't know everything, my dear. But I will tell you. Please listen."

He went back to the table and sat down. Francis brought the food in and sat the plates in front of them. He had made French toast, maple syrup, strawberries, and two sunny eggs on the side. Powdered sugar covered the dish.

Chapter 31

Two days later Emmaline and Robert arrived and the place seemed like a hundred guests had come to visit. There was chatter and excitement uncontained.

The first to spot them was Ginny. "Momma, there is two people outside getting out of Francis's automobile."

She opened the curtain to show her mother.

"I do believe it is the couple the men have been talking about. Quite striking the two of them."

"Let's go brother, come on!" She shouted and the two of them were on the staircase before their mother knew what happened.

Lilly smiled. She'd had some time to let all this news settle. It had been six or seven years that her life had been turned upside down, yet, she wondered if staying in the orphanage might have been better? She guessed not. Her kids were her heroes' every day she breathed and continued on. Get ready, she told herself. Family waited below.

Emmaline and Robert walked towards the house. Deuce told them that he would open the other house in a couple days. They didn't mind staying here until then he asked?

"No problem."

Jack ran fast and left his sister a few yards behind. "Whoa, hello!"

"We've been waiting for you. Are you Mr. Robert and Miss Emmaline, her fiancé?" *He spoke well for a three year old* thought Robert.

"Yes, we are. And who are you?" Asked Emmaline knowing exactly who they were. She couldn't help but smile. Her dream was coming true since she first thought of it as soon as her mother told her the whole story. *Incredible,* she thought.

"We are related, that's what momma says." Ginny spoke up and put her hand out to shake theirs.

Robert shook her hand and Emmaline did the same and then asked for a hug. She came low to the ground to be on her level and gave her a warm hug. Surprisingly, Ginny hugged back.

"Glad to meet both of you and yes, we are related. I can't wait to meet your mother."

"No more waiting. Here I am," said Lilly.

Emmaline stood and looked at the young woman

in front of her. "Finally."

"Emmaline, I've heard so much about you. I am happy to meet you. I have a sister."

"Lilly, yes!" She stood proud, waiting for this moment. "I'm sure Deuce and Francis filled you in as they have known me all my life."

Lilly smiled. She wasn't going to tell her about the father upstairs. He'd asked to save it for a day so that the two sisters could meet and get to know one another. She'd agreed.

"Let's all go inside. We can begin again." Robert said it well.

The next day after meeting her sister for the first time Emmaline felt light and without a care. She decided that they would all go to the lake and go swimming. Robert would watch out for the two little ones while the sisters caught up. It was a done deal. The chauffeur and gardener, Deuce and Francis, packed them a lunch and a drink. They included a nice blanket for a picnic. They expressed their desire they'd like to be going also!

Ginny and Jack took to the lake, and actually, both of them could do the freestyle or dog paddle. Their mother had taught them to float in a nearby lake on the property in Florida. Robert stayed close but relaxed slightly when he knew they had a few swimming skills. The sister laid out the blanket and readied it for a picnic for five. The sun was shining and it wasn't too hot. It would probably warm up in the late afternoon.

Emmaline started to tell her sister about the summers at the lake and the parties and explorations they used to take as kids. Lilly was intrigued, truly she wanted to know and see the pool. She had never ever seen a real pool. She'd only heard about them from Earl when he was in the fancier hotels or near the beaches in Miami. He had never taken her there for anything. She'd been to the local grocery store and maybe a clothing store in the local town. That was it.

"You've never seen a pool, the kind that is in the ground?" asked Emmaline.

"No, I haven't. Can we go and see it? Like you used to do."

"Yes, mom let's go and see. Please. We'll be real good," said Ginny. Jack shook his head in conclusion. He didn't want to miss this.

"Do you promise to be very quiet? There can be no yelling or laughing at all!" Robert issued.

"We can. We can. We do it all the time at home when dad is around."

Emmaline looked at Lilly. The expression on Lilly's face was blank, no emotion. Emmaline realized her sister was strong, probably stronger than herself.

"One sound and we all run. Do you understand? It is private property, though, there is no sign but still we don't want to intrude, at least for very long, anyway." Emmaline said.

"We'll go as soon as our picnic is finished." Robert was having fun watching the childrens' expressions. *It made it all the more fun* he thought.

Once they packed up, the adventure continued as the couple showed them how to get to the pool. They climbed up the ancient steps filled with green grass and old stone. It didn't crumble but the soft earth pushed in slightly with each step. Little boy Jack wondered out loud, "Do you think these steps lead to a fort or something?"

"What do you know about forts?"

"My mom told us about them. She pointed out the train window when we passed one near the ocean."

"You saw one?"

"We all saw it with our own eyes and it was gigantic, the biggest thing I ever saw."

"You saw the fort in Saint Augustine, right?"

"It was where we stayed overnight before leaving Florida and coming here," said Ginny.

"That is a big place Jack. You will probably study that in school, when you go someday, Jack." Robert tried to encourage him so he might remember what he saw.

As soon as they reached the top they all saw the pool. With big eyes they viewed the private pool. *Why was no one ever here* thought Robert? He just didn't have that answer.

Emmaline led them to the small storage shed and they looked inside. Lilly looked around and read a few labels on the boxes inside. *Puzzling* she thought.

Emmaline saw her staring at the boxes and asked, "What is it Lilly?"

"I'm not sure but something here looks familiar."

Robert lifted the box off the shelf and opened it to look inside. Then she saw the contents. She couldn't speak.

"Tell us Lilly. What is it? Have you seen this before?"

She shook her head yes. "Yes, I have."

She lifted a bottle out and remembered. "He brought one of these home one night and insisted I taste it, join him for a couple of drinks."

"What happened?"

"He drank more than half a bottle and passed out, not before he broke the bottle and cut himself. He blamed it on me."

"I'm sorry. You okay?"

"I'm fine. Why is this here? Do they make it

here?"

"I'm betting they do. However, lots of folks make this stuff, you know."

"I know, but this label bothers me. The guys that Earl hung with were not nice people, to say the least. Earl wasn't nice, either."

"Do you suppose we ask that reporter if he knows about this?" Emmaline asked Robert.

"I think that I should contact my dad at the paper, after all he sent the reporter down to see us in Saint Augustine.'

"A reporter? You mean the guy that gave me the chocolates from you?"

"The very one. He knows more than any of us, except maybe my dad."

"I think we best get going."

"Can we swim Miss Emmaline?" asked Jack.

"One dip and we're done!"

Chapter 32

Henry James Kelly was preparing his full length report, a weekend segment at his paper in D.C. He, of course, wrote this under a fictitious name. He had to be incognito now a days since Prohibition. It could get him killed and he knew that. His boss knew that and probably one or two organizations knew that. Who knew? He couldn't report every name he knew just the main guys of operation. Actually, from one week to the next things changed except the big mobs were grabbing more territory and killing off many who got in their way. Until, of course, someone new came to town and beat them at their own game. Lawlessness, restlessness, and swinging that would be music, song and dance. The country was on fire and that would be his title for the Sunday segment. It would include all the revelry, big time jazz artists, and places where people had a good time with the undercurrent and hint of the bad boys around town. Money and liquor, now that it was outlawed, seemed to be high stakes.

Caught in his thoughts, he was unaware that his secretary had delivered a telegram.

He opened it up and read it.

Hi Henry.

We wanted to thank you for delivering a very special package for us. It is with happiness that all is well. We wanted you to know that the recipient of such chocolates recalled the label from down south and has seen it next to our very own summer homes.

Worried,

Robert

"You don't say," he whispered aloud to himself. He made a phone call to Robert's dad.

"Interesting. Yes." That was all the man said over the phone.

Meanwhile, Ruth, Rose and little Lilly prepped for their summer vacation. They would arrive in a few days for a reunion with the Stephens and everyone would be there, except for Jack. He would be missed.

Lilly insisted they were bringing the cat, London and the dog, Petals. DJ would be coming as Garrett was already there having traveled aside Robert and Emmaline.

Charles and Mary Stephens would also meet them down there. Charles said he could take two weeks tops. That would have to do.

The day after the pool excursion Deuce and Francis told Emmaline and Robert, Lilly and her kids that they would be opening up the other summer home. The parties could then move over to the larger home.

After lunch Emmaline and Robert carried their items over to her summer home from her childhood. They walked inside and didn't get to the staircase.

Emmaline thought she saw a ghost and blinked her eyes, twice.

"Sir, you are dead. I mean you are not dead." Robert held on to the bags in his hand.

"It's me Emmaline. Robert, you are correct. I'm not dead."

"You. You are alive?" spoke Emmaline in a not distinct voice. She cleared her throat.

"I am alive."

"Mother buried you. Wait, Fitz buried you!"

"Please, Emmaline. I know you are shocked. Frankly, I am too. I finally get to see you after six long months."

"Oh Father, I missed you." Emmaline thought

she might faint, but too much had already happened.

Emmaline wasted no more time and ran to embrace her father after dropping her bags. She hugged him tight.

Robert set his bags down and smiled. "This is going to be quite a story!"

"Simple really," Jack Johnson teased.

"Simple?"

"Someone wanted me dead and they think I'm dead. So end of story."

"Not so fast," said Emmaline.

"Why?"

"Lilly, recognized a label yesterday and saw her husband drinking from it. He worked for people where she lived. Now he's dead and she escaped, barely."

"Ah, Lilly, you've met her I see."

"Yes, just yesterday. She's so lovely. Wait until you meet her. You'll love her. I already do."

"I did meet her the day before you arrived. I asked her to wait so you two could engage and learn about one another."

"Sweet, indeed."

"What about the bottles? Please explain and what does that have to do with Lilly?"

"Oh father, I think your neighbors sold liquor down south. Just like everyone else bootlegging but there's crime involved and murder, too."

"Please go on."

Robert continued the story and brought in the reporter with his story which involved Earl and his partner and how Earl ended up dead because he was going to compete with his boss. "Confusing, I know but Lilly saw the bottle labels and she's sure the same ones were handled by Earl and his bosses."

"I'm sure you're dad knows about this, right?"

"The better question is does my dad know about you?" Robert asked the inevitable.

"No, he doesn't. Not yet. I've kept this a secret so as to protect you and my family. There's so much chaos and shooting with all this bootlegging. I'm just remaining quiet for a while. I think I'll enjoy my expanded family while I'm at it," Jack Johnson answered.

"Sounds good."

"If you don't mind I need to make a phone call. After all bootlegging is still illegal in North Carolina." That was all he said.

The very next day the neighbors place was raided by six police cars with sirens and plenty of man power carrying loaded weapons, namely guns. It was all across the headlines. The property was now off limits, no swimming in the pool thought Emmaline.

Deuce and Francis were instructed to go to town

and purchase the major newspaper along with the national paper. They did as instructed and purchased a full load of grocery items for the coming summer reunion.

At dinner that night before they were served, Jack Johnson swiftly drew the paper through the air and landed it on the table before the others. "Headlines, take a look at what's happened!'

Headlines and pictures showed several people under arrest in front of the neighbor's house.

Emmaline scanned through the article and noticed another major article by James Winters, a reporter for the D.C. paper was on page twenty three. She quickly went to see the article. "Look Lilly, it's your place. It's a picture with the police there."

There was a picture of her deceased husband with his name, except they weren't ever really married so she was not named as next of kin. She sighed.

"What do I do? Anything?" she asked for advice.

"Sweetie, let me worry about everything. I'll talk with an attorney and make sure everything is handled properly. The abuse you suffered was tremendous beginning with the kidnapping and taking you far away."

"Does he have any money?"

"I'm not sure," she issued.

Later that night Robert called his father in New

York, not mentioning the presence of Jack Johnson, and told him about the bust down here. He already knew of it through his reporter friend, the very one that he and Emmaline had met.

"My friend the reporter from D.C. is coming to the summer home the same time as us. He wants to meet Lilly again."

"When are you coming?"

"Wednesday," Charles replied. "With your mother. She misses you."

"I cannot wait to meet up with you both. We have much to catch up on."

"Sounds great. We are staying two weeks, which is a lifetime in news," he added.

"It's going to be very special indeed, then," Robert answered. "Pearl is doing so good, dad. She has her own place which is quite busy. She books music and the place is always lively."

"She's a wonderful woman. I know she probably treated you quite well."

"Yes, she did. She helped quite a lot. She loves Florida by the way. So do I. We'll fill you in when you get here."

"Maybe you should reconsider running my paper down there in the Tropics. Just think about it."

"Dad, think about this. Seriously, you and mom might want to move down there and be near me.

Just think about it."

"You are trying to outwit me, I'd say."

"You know what they say?"

"No I don't. Tell me."

"Like father, like son." He waited for an answer. There was none. "Maybe if you move down there you can teach me to run a paper while I invent a couple things. Emmaline wants a hotel to run with Traveler Palms all around."

"Now, I have something to think about."

Chapter 33

The Reunion
After the headlines in the local paper it seemed there was daily national headlines about the gangsters and the killings and the speakeasies with all the liquor sales, not that it hindered the clubs, and it just became more known that the ban on liquor wasn't working. Everybody knew it, most people disobeyed the law. Even the law disobeyed itself. What was happening? It gave for plenty of discussions as the Johnson's had been in liquor sales for a long time.

Everyone at the summer homes relaxed and agreed that it was a good thing Jack escaped Chicago. The question was wouldn't someone come looking for him here? He didn't think so because they were too busy running New York, Chicago and expanding into new cities. There was an excitement in the air. Everyone felt it, especially the young and the female gender.

Wednesday came and the other parties arrived. "Won't mother have a heart attack or faint when she sees you?" asked Emmaline of her father.

"We'll have to ease her into it a bit. Fitz will be here, too. He'll help."

"We don't have to wait any further then, because the auto has arrived. Look," she said and pointed out the window.

Little Jack heard the whole conversation and for some reason he wanted to be the one to greet this lady, Emmaline's mother who he finally realized with all the chatter could have been his mother's mother or as Ginny spoke aloud, "Your grandmother Jacky!"

Out the door he flew and ran right up to her at the end of the path. He put his hand out and introduced himself, "Hello, I'm Jack. Nice to meet you Mrs. Johnson."

Taken aback but falling right in stride, "It's my pleasure Jack. How do you do?"

"I'm might fine, never been better, now that I'm here in North Carolina!"

"Oh, I see, you like it here," she replied. She smiled and decided to put herself down on his level, eye to eye.

He took his chance. He'd warn her so she wouldn't faint. "I have something to tell you so you won't faint when you get inside."

"Please, do tell."

"Your husband is alive. He's inside. He didn't die. Isn't that great news?"

She stared at him. Wondering. My, was he telling the truth?

"It's true. I'm not telling a lie."

"My husband is alive. What's his name?"

"Jack, just like mine," he answered very quickly.

"Well Jack, that is great news and I'm very happy that you are the one to tell me."

"You are welcome. Happy to tell you."

"Let's let them surprise me, shall we? We'll keep this a secret for just a short while. Okay?"

"Sure thing, let's go."

"Let's go," she said. She stood up. She was grinning ear to ear.

She held the little boys hand and they walked towards the summer home.

Later that day the Stephens arrived and with them the reporter named Henry James. They had picked him up in town just off the train. Fitz arrived the next day. Little Lilly came with her mother and Rose and her husband John. There was plenty to talk about. It seemed everyone had something going on in their life. Over the weekend the table was lively, friendly and informative.

A gaiety which lasted well into Saturday night.

Little Lilly planned a performance. She had been singing and dancing now in New York City and had refined her performances. At only seventeen she served up experience of that someone ten years older. Her family long ago decided she was made for it.

If the woman's Suffrage movement signified the long standing battle of equal rights, then Lilly took it ten times higher and faster. Nobody was going to tinker with her claim to stardom. For certain it was written in the stars that she saw every night. You wanted to vote she'd tell the women but I want to sing and be the best. She governed her own earnings which had been adding up quite significantly. Her accountant was John himself, a fair and honest man married to her sister.

Actually, he had discovered her and that is all he wanted from her. He told her that repeatedly. He wanted no money, nothing. She paid him when he got her new gigs or advanced her career. He also help with her contracts. In the end, she told him she relied on his advice and that was worth paying for.

"Put me at the best clubs," she'd say. "I want to do movies, please." She begged him. He looked out for her. A girl couldn't ask for a better business partner.

"You're dazzling Lilly. You don't even need me. I

think you can handle those New York sharks all by yourself. I know you could. But if it makes you feel better, I'm there for you."

"Thanks boss, don't leave me, ever. And get me a movie contract while you are at it."

"Sure thing, let's do it.

Saturday night after dinner at the Johnson's, attended by all, it was Lilly's time to show them her latest talents. She sequestered all the applause right after the first number. That night in the formal dining room would be a turning point for everyone present. Her talent succeeded in allowing the hearts and minds of those present that anything is possible with determination and talent. The joy in the room illuminated the night more than any bulb at the center of the ceiling, beyond the starry night outside, and Lilly's words and domination of sound and tone took that joy above their heads and physical bodies to a place one doesn't visit but once in their life. She was their Lilly, sister of the missing one.

Sunday came and the ladies gathered in the kitchen while the men retrieved a chair in the living room. The discussions centered on the plans. One by one they talked and support and encouragement were given.

Robert went first, "On our visit to Florida we were able to visit Mr. Edison's lab. He showed

Emmaline and I around and I was able to show him my portfolio. He was rather busy working on this and that. Since I've seen him I'm working on a walk in cigar room that holds numerous brands and keeps the tobacco fresher. I think that is one of my best ideas."

The men agreed to that idea. "I like that idea. What else have you got?"

"I'm working on some shoes, lighter in weight for the sands and places in the Tropics. Maybe I'll use some of the material he uses from his trees."

All the men agreed he should keep working on all his ideas.

"Emmaline wants to run a hotel." He said it and waited.

Silence.

"Why not?" He asked the men gathered.

"Partners is a better idea, don't you think?" asked Jack Johnson.

"Yes, I agree, partners. That is a big operation," said Charles Stephens. "Though, I do believe one could be a silent partner."

"Exactly. We don't have the money for a big venture but we could do it on a smaller scale." Robert explained.

"What about operating a newspaper down there in Florida?" asked Charles.

"Talk about inexperience. Dad I have none." Robert replied.

"I know. I was testing you. But we could be a silent partner and it could be a small paper."

"My fellow business man Ralph Heminger wants to invest in one of your ideas. He told me. He met you a month ago and was taken by your enthusiasm. He's an investor looking for new projects."

"He did tell me that," replied Robert. "Here's how I see it. We find property to build a small hotel, put a small newspaper inside and my lab will be in the back. Emmaline runs the hotel with her traveler palms and her sister Lilly works there for her until she decides what her future is. She has the kids so she needs income."

"I like the sound of this and remember I can come and work for you as a reporter. I told you I like it down there in Florida." Henry James offered his side of the entrepreneur game at hand. "Besides I have some money for Lilly. I happened upon it before the investigation took place. Earl had been saving for himself, it seems. I plan to give it to her here later today."

"Fabulous, she deserves it and you knew they would pocket every cent for themselves. What a time we live in, no one can keep up." Jack Johnson commented upon this unusual situation.

Charles spoke, "I'm in for a small paper down in

south Florida at your small hotel where Emmaline will manage the day to day. Buy extra property so that expansion is no problem. I'll teach you or maybe live there."

"What dad, really?"

"Not sure yet, I'm thinking about it."

"That's good news," Robert replied.

"I'm pretty sure the ladies will want to visit you for extended times. That would be Mary and Ruth. I have to keep a low profile, but they don't."

"How long do we have before this new venture begins?" asked Henry.

"It'll take about nine months for something small. There are lots of builders and supplies down there just waiting for the investors to start something new. I think the timing is perfect. I can write a contract for all of you," said John the lawyer.

"I'll call Ralph, he's the third silent partner. Jack, Charles, and Ralph will have an equal third with Emmaline and myself retaining a working partnership. Henry, we will employ you and until we get it going and you can stay at the hotel for free. Sound like a deal?"

"Yes, perfect. I'll maintain my status with the D.C. paper on a part time basis and part time with you. Makes perfect sense.

"Lilly, will have to make up her own mind but she has stated she wants to be near this family." Robert added.

Meanwhile the women talked about the two new

children that would now be a part of their lives. Little Lilly was ecstatic. She had a little niece and nephew and for her they were adorable. She was going to play with them all day long!

"Are you in love with Robert?" asked her mother.

Emmaline looked at her and replied honestly, "I didn't know if it would happen or not but it did. Yes, I am," she replied.

"When did you know?" asked Rose.

"Oh my. It happened at the most perfect time. We had just visited the Edison estate and there was a dock nearby with small boats. He told us to go for a row, if we knew how to row a boat. And so we did." She blushed. She remembered the most perfect moment and dreamed it all over again.

"You're blushing," said Mary. "Robert feels the same way about you."

"Thank you for having me here," Lilly spoke up.

"Lilly, we are so happy that Emmaline found you. Well, the reporter helped quite a bit." Ruth had never been happier.

"I am grateful for him. I want to be near all of you, forever," she said and began to cry. The women gathered around her and comforted her.

She stood and went to the large window facing the back of the property to the side of the kitchen. Her children watched her and remained seated but listened.

Emmaline went near her and looked out where she was looking.

Lilly June looked out the pane less window towards the vast and rolling untouched beauty before her. How did she get here? She turned and faced Emmaline and reached for her hand.

"If not for you, I'd be dead."

THE END

Thank you for reading Caroline Clemens historical fiction set in the 1920's in America. Her next project will be out soon. Check out the title *Three King Mackerel and a Mahi Mahi*, her debut Romantic Spy-Thriller!

Resource material for Chocolate for Lilly:

Cedar Point, the Queen of American Watering Places, Francis, David; Francis, Diane Mali, Amusement Park Books, Inc., 1995.

Last Train to Paradise, Standiford, Les, Crown Publishers, 2002.

Bohemian, Bootleggers, Flappers, and Swells, Carter, Graydon, New York, Penguin Press, 2014.

Poetry and Tales, Quinn, Patrick, Penguin Books, USA, 1978.

An Everglades Providence, Davis, Jack, University of Georgia Press, Athens & London, 2009.

Jazz, Giddins, Gary, DeVeaux, Scott, W.W. Norton & Co., New York, London, 2009.

End of Innocence, Time Life Edition, Britten, Loretta, Mathless, Paul, Richmond, Virginia, 2000.

The Iron Road, an Illustrated History of the Railroads, Volmar, Christian, Darling Kindersley Publishers, 2014.

On the web:

BabyCenter.com, eHow.com, History.com, SanduskyRegisterBlogspot.com, TheCompleteVictorian.com.